ROOK

DRAGON BRIDES
BOOK 11

KATE RUDOLPH

HE CAME to Earth to hunt fugitives… not claim a mate who sets his blood on fire.

Dragon Lord Rook is a warrior. He's deadly, disciplined, and done with the royal matchmaking games back home. To escape the meddling, he takes a mission on a backwater planet called Earth. Track the fugitives. Serve justice. Return to the stars.

Easy.

Until *she* crashes into his path.

Sasha thought the worst part of her week was running into her cheating ex. Wrong. Now she's on the run after witnessing a deal gone very, very wrong… and the only thing standing between her and death is a massive, muscled alien with eyes like fire and a growl that promises danger… and desire.

She's human. He's a dragon. It's an impossible match.

But Rook wants her beneath him, bonded for life.

Claiming Sasha means breaking every rule.

And losing her? *Unthinkable.*

Fated mates. Scorching heat. A possessive alien dragon who'll burn the universe down to protect what's his.

The Dragon Brides series brings all the steam, action, and heart you love—with a growly warrior who just met his match.

THREE MORE TOURS and Sasha would be home free.

The end-of-season quiet was creeping in, settling over the dense pine and fir she called her office.

Soon, the last of the tourists would pack up their brand-new, barely used gear and go home. She wasn't sure what she was going to do once she was no longer shepherding clueless Midwesterners or influencers so determined to get the perfect selfie they seemed intent on falling off a cliff.

The solitude was what she craved, what had drawn her to this life, but it also brought a familiar, low-humming anxiety. Too much quiet gave her too much time to think.

She definitely wasn't hiding in the gear shed.

That would be cowardice, and Sasha Forde was

no coward. She was merely taking a meticulous inventory of the equipment, her calloused hands moving with confidence over climbing ropes and carabiners. She hoped Erik would be gone by the time she finished.

They said not to date your coworkers.

That was true enough. It was even worse when that coworker you dated became an ex, especially in a place this remote. She wasn't sure what she had been thinking—a momentary lapse in judgment fueled by a shared bottle of whiskey and a lonely summer night.

Now it was clear: this tour company wasn't big enough for the both of them.

The heavy canvas flap of the shed's entrance rustled and slapped against its frame behind her. Sasha winced at the crunch of approaching footsteps on the gravel path. There was only one other person here today.

Erik Daniel. The ex.

Great.

"Hey, Sash, how you doing?" Erik asked. His voice was laced with a casual charm she now found grating, as if they hadn't both been studiously avoiding each other ever since she'd found him sneaking into Caroline's tent at midnight two weeks ago.

Sasha didn't turn from the wall of neatly coiled ropes. "Did you need something?"

"I know some of the stuff is heavy back here, babe. I thought you could use some help."

"Don't call me babe." It landed like a stone in the quiet shed. She hadn't liked it when they were dating; she liked it even less now.

"Come on, Sash. No need to be a hard ass." He stepped inside, letting the flap fall closed and plunging the shed into dusty, shadowed light. The air suddenly felt thick, too close. "I thought we were just having some fun. We were good together. We could still be good together."

"Erik, stop." She clutched a thick bundle of rope, holding it between them like a force field, a boundary he couldn't cross. "It's over. We're done. We don't need to do this, okay?"

"Why do you take everything so seriously?" he demanded, his tone shifting from wheedling to sharp. The friendly façade cracked, revealing sour resentment beneath.

And right then, Sasha remembered that they were alone, miles from civilization, and her cell phone's reception was spotty at best. Her heart gave a hard, sudden thump in her ribs.

Shit.

"I just want to get things ready for the tour," she said, her voice impressively steady. "Everybody's coming in a couple of days. It's fine."

Erik took another step towards her, his shadow swallowing what little light filtered through the canvas. She hated herself for the instinctual step back she took, the toe of her boot bumping against a stack of sleeping bags. Going deeper into the gear shed only meant she was more trapped.

Since when did she think of Erik as the type to trap her? She'd agreed to go out with him because he seemed nice, easygoing. Not this.

"You always think you're so much better than everyone else," he sneered. "So I made one little mistake. Get over it."

"How is Caroline?" Okay, that was bitchy, but she was allowed. She was the one that got cheated on.

Erik made a sound of disgust and turned on his heel, his anger a force in the small space. He shoved the canvas flap aside and stalked out of the shed, leaving Sasha alone with the silence.

Thank god. She let out a breath, the tension

draining from her shoulders. She really didn't want to deal with that anymore.

She got back to work, losing herself in the familiar rhythm of preparation. She tried to forget Erik was still around somewhere. He was infuriatingly decent at his job, almost as good of a guide as she was.

She wouldn't hate being on a tour led by him in other circumstances. He knew these woods well, and he had that infectious sense of adventure that made people come back year after year.

He even got better reviews than she did—a fact that galled her more than she cared to admit.

She was packing up her personal gear for the day, the late afternoon sun slanting through the trees, when she heard voices. A prickle of unease traced up her spine. She shouldn't have heard voices. Erik might be on a call, but, again, spotty reception. None of the rest of the team should be there. They were all on a multi-day hike far to the south and weren't due back for another two days.

Unless something went very wrong.

A lifetime of caution, of learning to listen to the subtle warnings the world gave her, made her move slowly. Something was off.

Erik wasn't in the main camp or in the small

gravel parking lot. His beat-up sedan was there, right next to her van, and there were no other vehicles.

So far not weird. So where was he? And why did she hear voices? Had she finally cracked from the isolation?

Hopefully not. Hearing voices in the woods was a totally normal thing, she told herself, a trick of the wind through the pines. But hearing them get louder and more distinct as she stepped farther down one of the lesser-used trails meant that they were real and definitely not a figment of her imagination.

"I can show you wherever you need to go," Erik was saying, his voice carrying clearly in the still air. "There's no one who knows these woods better than me."

That was debatable. She knew them just as well, if not better. But she wasn't going to interrupt this strange meeting to say so.

"Are you sure?" another unfamiliar voice asked. He had a strange, clipped accent, one she didn't recognize. In her line of work, she'd heard them all and had a pretty good ear for placement. This was different. Foreign, but not from any place she could name.

Sasha moved with stealth, her boots silent on the pine-needle-cushioned earth. She peered through the dense screen of greenery and saw Erik standing in a small, secluded clearing. He was surrounded by three men, all of them exceptionally tall and broad-shouldered.

They were dressed in dark, functional clothing that looked more tactical than civilian. Their posture was rigid, their presence radiating a quiet menace that made the hairs on her arms stand on end. One of them handed over a thick envelope. Erik took it, a greedy little smile playing on his lips as he weighed it in his hands.

Drug money? She didn't think Erik had that kind of sideline. Trail guides weren't paid well. Some weed on the side was one thing, but that fat stack was way more than a little weed. What was he into? Meth? Pills?

Her mind raced. Should she say something? Should she call the cops? Her phone was useless out there. She had no signal. Should she run away and pretend she didn't see any of this?

Yeah, that one. That was probably the best option.

Sasha took a careful step back, and her boot heel came down squarely on top of the only dry, brittle leaf in a three-mile radius. It cracked with a sound that seemed to echo like a gunshot in the suddenly silent clearing. She bit her lip hard to keep from cursing, her body tensing to stone.

She risked a glance back at Erik and his shady friends. Her blood ran cold. One of the tall strangers was looking right at her, his head tilted. His eyes, even from that distance, seemed to bore through the foliage, pinning her in place. They were an impossible, bright yellow, and for a terrifying second, she thought she saw them glow with an internal fire.

Oh, hell no.

He tilted his head. "Who is that?" he asked, his voice a low, dangerous rumble.

She wasn't going to stick around for introductions. She pivoted and ran, her survival instincts screaming. She heard Erik shout something after her, his voice tight with panic, but she couldn't make out the words.

Something scorched the air behind her, searing her back in a wave of intense heat.

Fire? Did they have flamethrowers?

What kind of drug dealers were they?

She didn't waste time looking back. She pumped her arms and ran like her life depended on it, because she knew with chilling certainty that it did. The forest floor, familiar beneath her boots, flew by in a blur of green and brown. Her lungs burned, her heart hammered in her ribs, but fear was a fuel more potent than oxygen.

She risked a single, fleeting glance over her shoulder, and what she saw made her stumble. A ribbon of flame was snaking through the woods behind her. It didn't spread or burn like a normal fire. It moved with a terrifying, liquid grace, like some sort of living entity that danced between the trees, incinerating ferns and vaporizing moss.

It had a mind of its own.

And it was coming for her.

2

ANYWHERE WAS BETTER than Vemion right now.

Rook reminded himself of that as a low-hanging branch thwacked him across the forehead, stinging his skin and nearly knocking his translator loose from behind his ear. He ducked, muttered a curse, and kept moving, only to have his boot land squarely on a slick patch of moss. He windmilled his arms, caught his balance by grabbing a sapling, and nearly wrenched his shoulder.

He gritted his teeth. The local flora on Earth was less forgiving than he'd expected, and the ground there, soft, uneven, riddled with tangled roots and the bones of old trees, seemed determined to turn his ankle with every step.

He could have been home.

He could have been sprawled out in one of his estate's sun-warmed gardens, a glass of spiced wine in hand, not a care in the world other than dodging the ever-watchful gaze of Shade, the Royal Matchmaker. Instead, there he was on that primitive planet, in a forest that smelled of wet earth and pine needles, with mud caked up to his knees and a headache pounding in his temples.

The worst part? He was trapped in his fragile human skin by the need for secrecy. No wings, no claws, no scales. It was like being half-alive, leashed.

He missed the weight of his dragon form, the stretch of his wings, the satisfying scrape of talons against stone. There, he was just a tall man in battered armor, indistinguishable from the locals if they didn't look too closely at his eyes—or, gods forbid, caught a glimpse of his smoking skin when he lost his temper.

Vemion wasn't perfect.

He could do without the endless rounds of court functions, the suffocating expectations of nobility, and the constant reminders from his mother that he was getting "dangerously close to an age where his prospects would dry up."

He'd made his choice. The alternative had been sitting through another excruciating tea with Shade and her endless parade of eligible dragonesses, all of them perfectly coiffed, perfectly mannered, and perfectly uninterested in anything except his title and the size of his hoard.

If he had to listen to her lecture about "potential brides" and "the importance of securing the bloodline" one more time, he'd scorch the velvet off the chairs. And then his mother would throw a fit, and Shade would redouble her efforts.

He was a dragon lord, a warrior. He didn't need a psychic's meddling or a list of handpicked mates. He'd find his own fate, thank you very much.

So there he was. On Earth. A backwater planet that, against all logic, had produced mates for more than one of his cousins. He was tracking fugitives from Vemion justice through a forest that, at a glance, looked almost like home.

The trees here were smaller, the air thinner, but there was the same green hush, the same sense of old, watchful things beneath the surface. The planet's sun was weaker than Vemion's, but it warmed his skin all the same. The birdsong was different, but it filled the silence between his footsteps.

At least he wasn't in a ballroom, forced to play the beast at some mating auction, watched by a hundred sharp-eyed dowagers and their calculating daughters.

Small mercies.

Something large and winged buzzed past his ear, making him flinch and slap at it instinctively. The insect ricocheted off his cheek, leaving a smear of something sticky behind. He grimaced, wiped it off, and scowled into the trees.

Why did the criminals never flee to the pleasure planets?

No, they always picked the places with the worst terrain, the thickest mud, and the most rules. They never picked somewhere with decent food or entertainment. Maybe that was the point.

He slowed, forcing himself to breathe evenly. He'd set up camp miles from there, relying on what little tech wouldn't seem out of place if discovered. His ship was hidden. He needed to stay away for now to protect it. His tracker, a battered, jury-rigged device shaped like a silver beetle, had given him a faint ping, leading him in this direction, but it was unreliable at best. The planet's magnetic field played havoc with Vemion sensors. Rushing would only get him lost, or worse, give away his position.

He paused, closed his eyes, and listened. The forest there wasn't silent, but the sounds were strange, no crackle of comms, no distant hum of anti-grav engines, just the hush of wind through pine needles and the soft, secretive rustle of small animals in the undergrowth. His nostrils flared, searching the air for anything out of place: the tang of fire, the hint of scorched metal, the chemical bite of interstellar weaponry.

Nothing but damp earth and the faintest trace of smoke.

He was about to move on when a woman's scream tore through the peace.

It was sharp, panicked, edged with desperation so acute it made the fine hairs on his arms stand up. Rook's head snapped east, every muscle going taut. He knew the sound of fear, real fear, the kind that meant blood and danger and death. The trail he'd been following led the other way, but there was no hesitation in his body.

Duty to protect was bred into his bones.

He ran.

Branches whipped at his face, leaving scratches along his cheekbones. The forest floor was a mess of rotting logs and slick ferns, and every step threatened to send him sprawling.

He felt slow, clumsy, like he was moving through water. If he could have shifted, if he could have called his wings, his claws, his fire, he would have been over these trees in seconds, a living shadow above the canopy. But there, he was just a man, and the knowledge gnawed at him.

He stumbled over a fallen branch, caught himself, and pushed harder. The scream echoed again, closer, brittle with pain or terror. He forced himself faster, lungs burning, anger and frustration hot in his chest. He was a dragon lord. He wasn't meant for this fragile body, this crawling pace. On Vemion, he would scorch a path through the forest, flame and fury clearing the way.

But on Earth, he was hidden.

He caught the scent of smoke, sharp and acrid, cutting through the green. It was more than just a trickle from a campfire: thick, biting, heavy with the promise of destruction. A dragon knew smoke. It was in his blood, an old friend, a comfort and a warning all at once.

On Vemion, the smoke from a dragon's fire meant home, meant safety, meant power. The scent would curl around him as he shifted, as he let loose the inferno inside him and watched it dance across the stones.

But there, in that damp, alien wood, smoke was an enemy. Someone was loose with their power, careless or cruel, and the world would pay the price for it. The air tasted bitter, stinging the back of his throat and making his eyes water.

He pushed forward, boots sinking into the soft ground, his mind racing. Where was the fire? Had his fugitives lost control? Or were they being careless, thinking no one would notice a little blaze in the middle of nowhere? His briefing had been clear: Earth's forests burned easily, their flora unaccustomed to dragon heat. The humans there didn't know how to handle real fire, not the way his people did.

But the ground was damp, the leaves slick from a recent rain. The fire shouldn't be spreading that fast.

He rounded a bend and skidded to a halt, the world narrowing to a single point.

There, flashing between the trees, a woman.

She was running, stumbling, her bright red flannel shirt a slash of color against the green. Her dark hair was pulled back in a messy knot, strands escaping to stick to her sweat-damp face. She looked up as she caught sight of him, her eyes wide, wild, too bright.

His body reacted before his mind caught up, a jolt of heat, a flare of protectiveness that had nothing to do with duty. The urge to shield her, to put himself between her and whatever hunted her, was immediate, overwhelming. Something in his chest twisted, sharp and unfamiliar.

She was human, yes, but there was something else, a pull he couldn't name, a sense that he'd been waiting his whole life to meet her there, in that moment, with the world burning down behind her.

"Get behind me," he ordered, voice low and rough.

The woman stared at him, frozen for a heartbeat, her chest heaving. He saw the flicker of calculation in her eyes. But whatever she saw in his face must have convinced her, because she scrambled toward him, boots sliding in the mud. She ducked behind his shoulder, close enough that he could feel the heat of her body, the frantic hammering of her heart.

"Do you work for the park?" she gasped, voice shaking. "There's—there ..."

She tried to say more, but the words tangled up, lost in another shuddering breath. Behind them, a wave of fire arced through the trees, a living ribbon of gold and red that devoured everything in its path. The heat was intense, almost physical, and Rook felt the old urge to answer it, to call up his own flames in response.

His fugitives.

Of course. Only a dragon could conjure fire like that, even there. But why were they hunting her? She was human, no threat to them.

It didn't matter. Right then, she was his to protect.

"Move."

3

THE PARK RANGER urged her back the way he'd come, acting like the fire was nothing more than an inconvenience, a brush-clearing project, not a living threat swallowing the forest.

Shouldn't he be calling it in?

Shouldn't he have a radio, a sense of urgency, a plan that involved more than just hustling her along a muddy trail?

"They had flamethrowers," she panted out, one boot scrambling for purchase as she vaulted over an old, moss-blanketed pine. "I think it's drug dealers, maybe. Or ... you do work for the park, right? Are you a cop?"

Her words came out in gasps, half carried by panic, half by the need to make sense of the impossible. He couldn't just be a regular hiker—not in that uniform.

She risked a look at him. His uniform wasn't right. It hugged his body, all black and slightly glossy. The material looked too sleek, too fitted, as if it were tailored to his broad shoulders and lean waist. There were panels of something that caught the light in flashes, and the seams looked reinforced, not stitched.

No patches, no name tag, no faded green or khaki like every ranger she'd ever known. He moved in the uniform easily, with a kind of grace she'd never seen on anyone in government-issued polyester.

It wasn't just the uniform that made her heart beat faster. Even with the panic thrumming beneath her skin, she couldn't help noticing how he filled it out. He was tall, at least a head above her, and built like he could haul a full-grown elk out of a ravine with one arm.

His jaw was all hard lines and stubble, his hair black and a little too long to be regulation, curling just above his collar. There was a heat to him, a presence that felt physical, almost magnetic. She felt it even with the fire behind them, even with her brain screaming at her to run. Her hands were shaking, but not entirely from fear.

He glanced at her, his strange yellow eyes catching the light for a split second. Her stomach knotted.

What the hell was wrong with her?

She was fleeing flamethrower-wielding drug dealers, and her heart was fluttering like a teenager's.

"I'm Rook," he said, his voice deep and rough, like gravel under tires. He hesitated before giving the name, as if he was leaving something off. Or maybe he wanted to say more—Captain Rook? Ranger Rook? Was it a last name or a first? Either way, he said it like it explained everything.

"Sasha," she replied, still panting. She could worry about the specifics later, when she wasn't running for her life. But if this guy was official, he needed to know what was happening. "They were talking to one of my co-workers, Erik." She didn't feel bad about throwing Erik under the bus, not after he'd cheated on her and certainly not now, with fire licking at her heels. "They handed him a big stack of cash. It could only be drugs, right?"

Rook nodded, but it was distracted, like he had a dozen other things on his mind. He didn't slow down, his eyes scanning the trees ahead.

Since when did a cop not care about drugs? Cops loved drugs.

Well ... okay, maybe that wasn't exactly right, but she'd watched enough procedural dramas to know that "mysterious fire in the woods, possible drug deal, ex-boyfriend getting paid off" should at least merit a little more than a nod.

She pushed herself to keep up, legs burning. Her lungs were tight, not just from fear, but also exhaustion. She'd spent the whole afternoon hauling gear, restocking first aid kits, checking bear canisters, and prepping for the next round of tourists. Her arms ached from lifting heavy packs, and her back twinged every time she dodged a low branch. Sweat trickled down her spine, sticky and cold against her shirt. It was getting harder to push one foot in front of the other, but the memory of that living ribbon of fire kept her moving.

Rook didn't seem to feel it at all. He moved with an easy, relentless stride, barely winded, his boots barely making a sound on the pine-needle carpet. The way he moved all effortlessly made her hate him a little.

"Wait!" she called as Rook veered left, cutting through a patch of ferns.

He stopped instantly, turning back to her, eyes narrowed in question. "What?"

"There's a gorge that way," she said, trying to catch her breath. Her ribs ached. "We'll be trapped. Everyone knows that."

For a moment, he just looked at her, as if weighing her words, then gave a single, sharp nod. "Lead the way," he said.

She didn't hesitate. Pushing past him, she headed back toward camp. If they could just make it to the parking lot, to her van, maybe even to the old satellite phone stashed in the emergency locker, they might have a chance. Rook didn't try to stop her, just fell in, matching her pace exactly.

They crashed through a thicket of young saplings and broke onto a narrow, well-worn trail. Sasha's pulse pounded in her ears, the sound almost drowning out the distant roar of the fire. She could feel the heat licking at her back, the air shimmering with it, but she kept her eyes forward, focusing on the trail, the next step, the next breath.

Then a shadow flickered ahead, stepping onto the path with a confidence that made her blood run cold.

It was one of the drug dealers. Up close, his uniform looked familiar. The same dark, high-tech material as Rook's, the same tight fit over a frame that was all muscle and menace. His boots were heavy, but he moved with the same predatory grace. There was something wrong with his eyes, too, something flat and inhuman.

The man's mouth twisted into a grin that showed too many teeth. "The great Rook? What a surprise." His accent was strange, clipped, like he was trying to mimic a language that didn't quite fit his mouth.

He lifted one hand and, as casually as if he were flipping a coin, conjured a ball of flame.

Sasha blinked, her mind stuttering to a halt.

The fire didn't go away. It just sat there, hovering in his palm, the color richer and hotter than any campfire she'd ever seen. No lighter, no fuel, no trick. She stared, waiting for the illusion to reveal itself, for the wires or the special effects.

Nothing. The flame just grew, licking up his forearm, illuminating the sharp angles of his face.

What? It had to be fake. People didn't just conjure fire, not outside of YouTube prank videos. Maybe a magician could do it, but this wasn't a party trick. This was ... she didn't even know. And the flame wasn't dying down. If anything, it was getting bigger, brighter, hungrily reaching for the sky.

"Get behind me, Sasha," Rook said, his voice calm.

She didn't need to be told twice. Ducking behind him, she put as much of his body between her and that impossible fire as she could. Her hands trembled, her knees threatening to buckle. She pressed her palm to the solid wall of his back, felt the heat rolling off him, and realized she'd never been more grateful for a human shield in her life.

What the actual hell was happening?

Branches snapped behind them. The other drug dealers emerged from the trees, fanning out to block the trail. Erik stumbled after them, face ashen, eyes wild. His shirt was askew, his hair a mess; he was clutching the envelope of cash like it was a life raft.

Now that she could see them all together, the similarities were impossible to ignore. The uniforms, the stature, the strange, glowing eyes. They looked less like a drug gang and more like a squad of mercenaries from a sci-fi movie, except the terror was real, and the fire was very, very real.

"How are you doing that?" Erik demanded, voice wobbling dangerously close to a whine. He stared at the fireball, his expression a mix of greed and fear, the kind of look he used to get when he was about to make a bad decision.

Had she really dated him? Had she really ever found that kind of weakness attractive?

Though, in fairness, she wanted to know, too. She just wouldn't beg for answers.

"No witnesses," one of the dealers said, his words flat and final, like a judge delivering a sentence.

The fire-wielder shrugged, almost bored, and tossed the ball of flame directly at Erik. It hit him square in the chest and flared outward, engulfing him in an instant. It was too fast, too complete, nothing like the movies with their slow-motion agony.

Erik went up like dry tinder, the flames swallowing his scream before it could fully form. There was a smell, sharp, acrid, not quite like burning meat, more like scorched hair and melted plastic. The blaze flashed blue for an instant, then guttered out, leaving nothing but a blackened husk crumpled on the trail.

Sasha screamed, the sound tearing out of her throat raw and wild. Her legs gave out, and she landed hard on her knees, hands pressed to the earth. Her heart jackhammered in her chest, and her vision blurred, the world swimming between horror and disbelief.

Oh god. She was about to die. This was it. Her story was going to end in a forest, burned alive by monsters pretending to be men.

Rook stepped forward, his posture shifting. Something in him changed, the air around him growing impossibly hot. He held out his hands, palms open, and the flames swirling in front of the drug dealers seemed to hesitate, as if waiting for his command. For a moment, he looked like a circus performer, a fire-eater or an illusionist, but the power radiating from him was too real, too raw.

He was one of them.

No witnesses.

The words rattled in her skull, echoing in the same emotionless voice as the man who had just incinerated Erik.

She was the only living witness.

And she wasn't going to let them burn her up.

Sasha scrambled to her feet. Her muscles screamed in protest, but she ignored the pain. She turned, picked a gap in the trees, and ran. Branches whipped at her face, but she didn't care. She ran like her life depended on it.

Behind her, she heard Rook shout something, his voice a guttural snarl. Heat flashed, brighter than the sun, and the roar of fire chased her through the woods. Sasha didn't look back. She forced her burning legs to keep moving, her arms pumping, her breath coming in short, ragged gasps. The forest blurred past, a smear of green and brown and shadow. All that mattered was the next step, the next patch of ground, the hope that maybe she could outrun the impossible.

She wasn't ready to die. Not there. Not then.

Not like that.

4

THIS WAS A MESS.

Rook shot flame at the nearest fugitive. Fire roared from his palm in a bright, searing arc that split the darkness and threw wild shadows across the trees.

But the man was a skilled wielder, quick and practiced. He caught the attack with his own fire. The two flames collided, hissing and twisting in the air before sputtering out with a sharp, acrid pop. The smell of scorched bark rose around them, thick and bitter, clinging to Rook's tongue.

Even with the recent rain, if they fought fire for fire in those woods, there would be a conflagration. Flames would leap from pine needle to moss, racing through the undergrowth until the whole forest was a blackened scar. He could already feel the heat building in the air, a warning that pressed tight against his skin.

Damned flammable planet.

The trees there burned too easily. The air was too dry beneath the canopy.

The fugitives seemed to sense the same danger. They moved with a strange, predatory grace, slipping between the trees with the silent confidence of men who had spent too long on the run. Rook watched one of them flare his hands, conjuring a quick flash of fire that spun between his fingers like a coin. It was a taunt, a show of power meant to distract. Another let out a low, rasping laugh, the sound curling around the trunks and echoing in the growing gloom.

The tallest of the group, broad-shouldered with a scar running from his jaw to his temple, lifted his chin. He met Rook's gaze, his yellow eyes shining in the dusk, and tipped an invisible hat in mockery before melting back into the gathering darkness. The others followed suit, their movements efficient and practiced. One flicked his wrist, sending a spark whistling through the air before vanishing behind a fallen log. Another stepped backward into the shadows, the fire in his palm shrinking to a pinprick before it winked out.

In less than a minute, the entire group was gone.

The forest swallowed them. The only sign of their presence was a faint crackle in the underbrush and the lingering scent of burned resin.

Rook cursed as the last one disappeared. He could give chase, but he was no fool. He would not run into an ambush. There had been at least a half dozen in the attack, and no doubt more were waiting.

Slavers didn't work alone. They traveled in packs, covering each other's backs, always ready to spring a trap.

His paperwork hadn't mentioned it, a typical bureaucratic oversight, but he recognized two of the men from past run-ins. The one with the scar had a reputation for cruelty and cunning. There were only so many reasons dragons might come to Earth to regroup. The planet was rich in minerals, yes, but nothing so rare it couldn't be found elsewhere in the galaxy.

People, though.

People were always worth something to slavers. Humans who had no idea the universe teemed with predators who would use them up and discard their withered husks were easy prey. They fetched a high price on the black market.

He closed his eyes for a second, listening to the faint echo of the fugitives' laughter. Slavers. He'd known it as soon as he saw their eyes, their posture. Too confident, too cold.

And the woman, Sasha, was somewhere in those woods, more vulnerable than anyone. She'd run off on her own, panic and survival instinct driving her deeper into the dark. She didn't know what hunted her, not really.

He spared a glance for the human the slavers had murdered. Now, he was nothing more than blackened bones, dragon fire having devoured everything within him. In another few minutes, he'd just be dust. The faint, sickly-sweet smell of fat and flesh burned to nothing hung in the air. Rook pressed his lips together, jaw clenched.

Another crime to add to the slavers' tally.

He turned away, refusing to linger. More lives were at stake than a fool who'd sold out his own kind for a handful of credits.

Rook spared one last glance down the slavers' path, his senses straining for movement. They wouldn't leave the planet just because they knew he was hunting them. Besides, they couldn't leave until the planetary convergence in six days. The window for transit was narrow, dictated by the complex dance of stars and gravity wells. Until then, they were trapped there.

So was Rook, for that matter.

He listened for signs of Sasha. The woods pressed in close, shadows thickening as the last light faded. Darkness was falling, the kind of black that swallowed sound and blurred the edges of everything. The wind had died, leaving the forest heavy and silent, broken only by the distant call of an owl and the soft drip of water from branches overhead.

He summoned flame and held it before him, a pale orb hovering above his palm. The fire flickered, chasing back the dark, but it wasn't enough. The trees hunched close, their trunks swallowing the light, and every branch seemed to move with a life of its own. He moved slowly, his boots squelching in the damp moss, eyes straining for a flash of movement, an echo of breath.

His instincts raged, screaming at him to find her. To protect her. He wasn't sure what else.

There was a pull in his chest, sharp and insistent, that had nothing to do with duty and everything to do with the strange, electric awareness he'd felt from the moment she crashed into his life. His hands tightened, the flame in his palm flaring brighter.

He caught up to her at a small stream, the water rushing over smooth stones in a quiet, bubbling song. She crouched on the far bank, eyes wide and wild in the firelight. When she saw him, she jerked upright and hurled something dark his way.

Rook dodged, his body moving on instinct, but as water rained down over him, cold and sharp, soaking his collar, he realized it wasn't a weapon.

It was a canteen. The cap clattered across the pebbles, rolling to a stop at the edge of the stream.

He squashed his fire, letting the light gutter out, and held his hands up in what he hoped was a gesture of surrender. The world snapped back to near darkness, the only illumination a thin silver band from the rising moon and the gleam of the stream at his feet.

Sasha was panting, her shirt smudged with dirt, her hair coming out of its tie in wild, tangled waves. Her cheeks were streaked with grime, and a scratch high on her jaw was bright with fresh blood. She looked wild and beautiful, as fierce as any creature he'd ever hunted.

And that was certainly not the time to notice.

His dragon didn't give a damn about timing. His heart thudded heavily in his chest, each beat echoing in his ears. A low, electric awareness vibrated under his skin, a restless heat that made his palms itch. His eyes traced the curve of her throat, the rise and fall of her chest as she tried to catch her breath. She was a mess, but the wildness in her eyes and the stubborn set of her jaw sent a surge of protective possessiveness through him.

"You're one of them!" Her voice hit him like another splash of water, cold and accusatory.

"I assure you, I am not." He took a step closer, careful to keep his hands up, palms open and empty. She held her ground, feet braced on slick river stones. Probably because another step back would put her in the stream, and he doubted she'd risk a tumble with him so close.

"You ... How did you ... What's going on?" Her voice shook, but she didn't back down. If she had another canteen, he was certain he'd be doubly soaked.

"I am sorry you have been mixed up in this," he said. "Those men are slavers from my home planet. I am hunting them to bring them to justice."

"Planet?" Her voice rose with disbelief. "You're a freaking alien? But you look ..." She trailed off, her eyes raking over him, searching for something otherworldly.

He would have shifted forms if he had the space or the time. He refrained from summoning fire again. She'd seen it once. She knew. She just had to get over the shock. He felt a pang at revealing his secret, but he had little other choice. Unlike the slavers, he wasn't going to murder a witness. Who would believe her, anyway?

"You are in grave danger," he warned. He let the words hang, heavy and honest.

She stared at him, every muscle tense. "How can I even understand you if you're from another planet?" Her suspicion was sharp, but underneath it, he heard the tremor of fear.

He tapped a spot behind his ear, then under his throat. "I have translators. So do the fugitives. They are common for intergalactic travelers."

"Intergalactic. Oh my god." She pressed a hand to her forehead, fingers trembling. The moonlight caught the edge of her jaw, the scratch there dark and vivid.

He needed to keep them moving. "You are in danger," he repeated, his voice more urgent. "Those men will either kill you or try to capture you. I give you my word as a Dragon Lord that I will not let that happen."

She stared at him, blinking rapidly. Each breath quickened, fogging in the cool night air. "Lord? As in, what, god?"

"Do you not have lords here?" He was sure he'd

read something about them on this planet, though his dossier had been scant.

"I guess in England. Not here in America." She straightened, shoulders squaring, breathing growing steadier. "So you're saying there are a bunch of asshole slavers in these woods and you're chasing them."

"Yes."

"Erik was their guide."

"How do you know that?" He stepped closer, the question clipped and direct.

"Because I overheard them. And they gave him money. I thought it was drugs, but this is even worse. You need my help." Her tone shifted mid-sentence, from outrage to something almost businesslike.

That brought Rook up short. "Excuse me?"

"You're stumbling around these woods like a confused CEO from the city on a weekend getaway with his mistress. I practically live in these woods. If you want to find these fuckers, you need my help." She crossed her arms, daring him to argue.

Did he? Rook thought he'd been doing fine on his own. But he didn't want this woman wandering alone, not with slavers still out there.

His gaze dropped to her hands. They were still shaking, just a little, but her grip was steady. A stubborn fire burned in her eyes, the kind he'd seen in warriors who refused to surrender. He felt the pull again, low in his gut.

He could agree to this, at least until he could find a safe place for her.

"I accept." He kept his voice low and measured, but a note of finality in it brooked no argument.

For a moment, they just stood there. The stream rushed between them, and the forest crowded close and silent. The moon climbed higher, silvering her hair and throwing his shadow long and thin across the water.

She nodded once, sharp and determined. "Good."

He found himself smiling, just a little, despite everything. There was more steel in this woman than in most soldiers he'd met.

Rook stepped across the stream, his boots splashing in the cold water. She didn't flinch when he closed the distance, just watched him with wary, unblinking eyes.

"We need to move," he said quietly. "If they regroup, they'll come for us."

"Then let's go," she replied. "But you're following me this time."

5

SHE WAS LEADING a dragon through the woods. Of all the clients she'd ever guided, counting at least three different cults, this one was definitely the weirdest.

Sasha moved by memory. The night pressed in, cool and heavy. A dense canopy swallowed the moonlight, leaving only trembling silver ribbons pooled on the moss and roots below. She didn't need more than that. Every turn, every dip in the ground, felt as familiar as her own home in the dark.

Still, her nerves hummed with an uneasy sharpness. Somewhere out there, men who weren't men prowled the shadows.

Slavers. Dragons.

Aliens.

Whatever she called them, the danger was the

same. Her mind cataloged every stray snap in the underbrush, every gust of wind that didn't sound quite right. There was a strange comfort from the hulking shape at her back.

Despite the danger, she couldn't remember the last time she'd felt that safe with another person in the wild. She had built her life on not trusting anyone, on being the one who looked out for herself. Now, with Rook, the fear wasn't quite so sharp.

A branch snapped under his boot, and he cursed in a language she didn't recognize, a string of harsh, guttural sounds. She glanced back just in time to see him stumble over an unseen root.

"I am summoning my fire," he warned, his voice tight with irritation. "Don't be frightened."

"Don't," she snapped, sharper than she intended. The memory of that living fire snaking through the woods sent a shudder up her spine. "It'll ruin your night vision."

Rook made a low sound of protest, the noise of a man used to being obeyed. She could practically feel the tension in his jaw, the muscles bunching in his powerful neck. He swept past her, his long stride eating up the trail. She had to scramble to keep up, her mind flicking between watching for danger and fighting the urge to argue with him. This was her territory. She sure as hell wasn't letting some big, fire-breathing alien lead her into a trap.

"I'm leading," she reminded him, her voice flat.

He didn't slow. "I know where my campsite is," he grit out.

Pride. Stubbornness. It matched her own in a way she found both aggravating and, god help her, almost funny.

"It is my responsibility to ensure your safety," he insisted, his voice pure steel and command, every inch the dragon lord he claimed to be.

"Same," she tossed back, lifting her chin. Let him puzzle that one out.

He muttered something very unlordly under his breath, a sound that raked down her spine in an entirely too-pleasant way.

Why did her body react like that? It had to be some kind of panic response, her system short-circuiting before it all went to hell. She shut the thought down and focused on the path.

Rook fell into step beside her, a silent truce hanging in the air. Every so often, she felt the prickle of his attention as he glanced her way. It was protective and assessing, but also strangely tentative, as if he worried she might disappear if he blinked.

Ahead, the ground sloped gently upward as the

trees thinned. Sasha recognized the small clearing before they even reached it, a hidden spot just off the main trail.

"It's just over here," Rook announced, striding ahead of her as if he'd been graciously letting her lead all along. He ducked under a low branch and stepped into the open space.

His camp was stark. The tent looked like a prop from a sci-fi movie, all slick black material and sharp angles with no visible zippers or poles. It was a compact dome, staked with military precision and barely big enough for a man of his size. A ring of stones marked a fire pit, but it held only cold ash. The site was immaculate. Even a man who could conjure flames from his fingertips took fire safety seriously.

She stepped closer, scanning the quiet clearing. A cold foreboding teased the back of her mind.

Rook's hand shot out, his fingers closing warm and strong around her forearm. The grip was firm but not painful. She froze, her pulse skipping.

"Someone's been here," he said, his voice a low rush of tension.

Before the words could register, shadows exploded from the tree line. Two of the fugitives appeared, their faces twisted in snarls as they conjured swirling balls of fire between their hands. Sasha's instincts took over, and she threw her arms up as if she could block the attack.

In the same instant, Rook shoved himself in front of her. He threw up a wall of his own fire with a roar. His flames met theirs, swallowing the attack with a deafening hiss. Wind and heat slammed into her, stealing the air from her lungs. The light illuminated everything: the furious faces of the slavers, the gleaming edges of the tent, and every drop of sweat on Rook's brow.

Then a third slaver slid from the darkness behind them, cutting off their escape. He was leaner than the others, his mouth curved into a predatory grin that never reached his golden eyes.

"Lord Rook even brought us a present," the man sneered, his gaze raking over Sasha. "We owe you, truly." The words made her skin crawl.

Fear had no time to set in before the clearing erupted into violence.

Rook shoved her sideways, a surprisingly gentle push that sent her stumbling toward the cover of a broad pine tree. "Take cover!" His voice was sharp as a gunshot, a raw, protective sound that told her he would stand between her and hell itself.

She scrambled behind the gnarled trunk and

crouched low, her heart hammering against her ribs. The bark dug into her palms. She watched slivers of the fight through the branches: blasts of fire arcing like molten arrows, Rook twisting and casting out ribbons of heat, the slavers splitting, then converging.

The image of Erik flashed through her mind, his body vanishing in a blast of blue-hot flame. Her stomach clenched. She forced the bile down and pressed her forehead to her knees, taking a single, ragged breath. She would not break.

The fight turned. One of the slavers hurled a spinning orb of fire straight at Rook. He moved to deflect it, but a second bolt struck him from the side. The impact sent him staggering to one knee. He caught himself with a snarl, the acrid scent of singed fabric filling the air.

Oh no. They were *not* doing this. She should have been paralyzed. She should have stayed hidden. But watching Rook fall ignited something wild and furious inside her.

Her eyes scanned the ground, and her hand closed over a rock the size of a softball. It was rough and cold, its weight a surprising comfort. She didn't think. She just reared back and threw it with every ounce of adrenaline-fueled anger in her body.

The rock caught the nearest slaver square in the cheekbone with a satisfying thunk. The big man crumpled sideways, his conjured flame sputtering out.

Her jaw dropped. She didn't have time to be surprised. Her hand was already closing around another stone, a lopsided chunk of quartz. She threw it wildly, but the distraction was enough.

Rook surged to his feet, power shimmering off him in visible waves. He lifted his hands, his palms blazing with a ferocious light, and sent a sheet of fire straight at the slavers. It was controlled and precise, a blade of heat that cut through the clearing. One slaver went down with a howl, his body engulfed. The other, seeing his allies felled, turned and ran.

Heat and silence crashed down. For a long moment, all Sasha could do was breathe, the coppery taste of fear thick in her throat.

She broke cover and darted to Rook's side. He stood over the unmoving slaver, blood still trickling from the mark her rock had made.

"Is he dead?" she whispered, her voice scratchy.

"Yes," Rook said, his gaze fixed on the body.

"Good," she replied, fierce satisfaction warring with a tremor of shock.

She looked up at Rook. Fresh beads of sweat slid

down his temples. He pressed a hand to his shoulder where the attack had landed, his breath coming in shallow bursts. Smoke curled from the singed fabric of his shirt. The sharp, sour smell of burnt skin tangled in the air. He was hurt.

Blood welled along the seam of his sleeve, a dark stain spreading. He was trying to hide the pain, but she could see it in the tight clench of his jaw. The remaining slavers knew where they were. It was only a matter of time before they came back.

She took a breath that was all char and pine needles. "Come on," she said, her voice steady. She slid an arm under Rook's good side, forcing him to lean on her. "I know a place we can go."

He straightened, letting just a little of his weight rest against her. She half walked, half dragged him away from the ruined camp and deeper into the safety of the woods.

SASHA WAS DOING her best not to think about the evil dragons in the woods.

A twig snapped. She nearly jumped out of her skin, her hand flying to her chest where her heart was pounding. She bit back a curse, squeezing her eyes shut to steady her frantic breathing. The night felt closer there, thick and electric, every creak of the forest feeding her paranoia.

She was failing miserably.

Rook's breathing was getting heavier. He grunted every time they had to clamber over a fallen log or up a challenging hill. Whatever had hit him was taking its toll, and she did not need a dead dragon on her hands, at least not the one *good* dragon she could find.

Every so often, a crunch in the brush or a shiver

through the leaves made every muscle in her body tense. The woods felt haunted, as if shadows watched her from behind every tree. Her mind kept flashing back to Erik, to the burst of blue flame that had devoured him alive. The smell of burnt hair. That sickening second where her brain insisted it was a special effect, not reality. Alien or not, this was her world now, and its rules had been torched right along with the rest of her night.

They really needed to update the guide manuals. She had no idea how to handle this situation.

Her feet crunched through another patch of dry leaves. The trees opened up, offering a wider slice of the stars. She could make out a twisted blue ribbon curling overhead, the Milky Way stretched above the tips of the pines. Instead of filling her with awe, the open sky only made her feel exposed.

A rustle in the underbrush, quieter than the last but closer, made Sasha press her lips together to bite back a scream that was half panic and half reflex. Her fingers curled tighter around the bag slung over her shoulder. Maybe she could whack a dragon with it.

"That's not them," Rook assured her, his voice a low rumble at her back. "These fugitives move in silence."

"So we won't hear them before they kill us?" Her voice was thin, rough with nerves.

His footsteps splashed in a puddle behind her as he moved closer. "I will not let any harm come to you."

It would have been more reassuring if his voice wasn't tight with pain. Even simple words seemed to cost him, each syllable clipped. She could hear how much it hurt him just to walk, every labored breath sharper than the one before.

She pushed on, leading them through the undergrowth, praying every choice was not the wrong one. Her mind raced. An old logging road? Too open. The stream? A potential trap. The only safe place was somewhere with walls.

After five more minutes of picking their way through a thick, black clump of firs, they broke into a sudden clearing. Moonlight spilled across a patch of tall grass. At its center stood a sturdy little cabin that looked more dilapidated than she knew it was.

Broken windows peered out from the log walls like dark, watchful eyes. Leaves and pine needles piled in forgotten mounds against the porch. The skeleton of a silent wind chime swayed from the eave.

"This is an old ranger's station," she said. "They

don't use it anymore, but it still has running water and walls. Campers mostly sneak up here to have sex now." She bit her lip.

She should *not* think about sex and Rook in the same sentence.

Except she was.

She could blame adrenaline or the way her body vibrated with leftover terror, but that was a lie. Some reckless, traitorous part of her brain kept spinning wild what-ifs.

Was his mouth as hot as his breath? Would his hands be careful or hungry? She must be losing her mind. Apparently, almost dying triggered the world's least convenient crush. She chalked it up to hormones, panic, and the knowledge that tomorrow was not a guarantee.

"This place is ..." He trailed off, taking in the half-collapsed porch and dirt-encrusted windows.

"Not up to your standard, my lord?" She shot him a sidelong glance, every word dripping with sarcasm.

For a second, Rook looked genuinely affronted. His lips pressed into a thin line, and he straightened, a flicker of dragon stubbornness in his posture. "I have slept in far worse environments."

Sasha steeled herself, shoved the door open with

a wince at the squeal of the hinges, and stepped inside. Dust motes danced in the sliver of moonlight. The cabin was empty except for a scarred wooden table, a pair of ancient benches, and a battered sink. No rodents scattered. The air smelled of old wood and the sharp, sweet scent of pine.

"There." She gestured, ushering Rook to the nearest bench. He moved as if his injuries were weighing him down, steps heavy and careful. The moment he sat, the invisible thread holding him together seemed to snap. His shoulders hunched, his head dropping forward.

Sasha rushed to his side and crouched, her hands flying to his face. His skin was feverish, slick with sweat. "Hey. I need you to stay awake, okay? Eyes open."

His eyes fluttered open, pupils wide in the gloom. He stared at her. "Your eyes are green."

It was just a fact. But his voice held a dreamy quality, as if the pain had dulled all his edges except for this one tiny detail.

Sasha very sternly told her heart not to flip over. The man was hanging on to consciousness by a thread. If he passed out, she did not know what she would do. Even if she could get a signal, she doubted a hospital could treat him.

Hello, 911? Yes, I have a magical alien dragon lord passed out in the old sex-cabin in the woods. No, I didn't give him such a good lovin' that he passed out. You see, there are also magical alien dragon slavers after us.

Oh, you think I need to be committed? Yeah, me too.

She forced herself into motion, yanking open the cupboard beneath the sink. A battered first aid kit was stuffed inside. She twisted the sink's tap. A shudder in the pipes, a cough, then cold, clear water gushed out. Sasha nearly moaned in relief. She found a battery-operated lantern in a drawer, and its dim, golden light made the cabin feel fractionally safer.

When she returned to Rook, he was hunched over, his ribcage shuddering. Sweat beaded on his brow. He tried to sit up straighter, his eyes a bit less glassy but still on the edge.

"I'm guessing dragons don't have magical healing powers," she said, needing to get him talking. Her hands snapped open the plastic latches on the kit. "Is there anything I should avoid? Silver? I don't have a pile of gold to sit you on to make you feel better."

"Why would that make me feel better?" he groaned.

He was talking. That was good. She knelt beside him. "Don't dragons have hoards of gold?"

"Not this dragon." He shifted and let out a sound of pain, one hand pressed to his wounded shoulder. The movement twisted his shirt, exposing the angry, blistered gash beneath.

Sasha placed her hand on his knee, grounding herself. "Stay still. Let me."

"There is a healing salve in a pouch on my belt. It will ease the pain."

All she had were antiseptic wipes and a flimsy bandage. Healing salve sounded wonderful.

She reached for it, practically wrapping her arms around his body. His torso was impossibly hard beneath her forearm, heat rolling off him in waves. His scent, a mix of burnt fabric, woodsmoke, and something undeniably male, filled her head. For a second, the world telescoped down to the closeness of them, her chest pressed to his side, the soft whoosh of his breath in her ear.

They froze. She felt the rise and fall of his chest, the hitch when he realized how near she was. Their gazes locked. Rook's eyes flicked to her mouth, hunger and restraint warring in their green-gold depths.

Sasha licked her lips, nerves and want spinning

together. She fumbled for the pouch and edged back, her heart hammering. The cool air felt sharp after the heat of him.

He was injured. He was in her care. But he was also a dragon lord from outer space.

She unscrewed the cap of the salve. The stuff inside was a pale, glistening green, with a scent like crushed pine needles and eucalyptus. She dipped her fingers in. It was cool and slippery, like aloe.

She nudged his shirt off his shoulder. The burn stretched over his upper arm, threaded with angry red lines. Her stomach lurched. She touched the salve gently to the wound. Rook jerked, muscles tensing, then relaxed with a rush of relief. A deep, guttural groan escaped him, a sound so low and rough it bordered on sexual.

The sound shot through her, pooling deep in her gut. Her skin prickled. Every brush of her hand suddenly felt like it might catch fire.

"Sorry," she mumbled.

He shook his head, jaw tight, but his look was pure heat.

She finished applying the salve with slow, careful strokes. "There," she said, her voice softer now. "You'll be good as new in no time."

Their gazes found each other again, hers swimming with nerves, his heavy-lidded and bright with something sharp and greedy.

Did she lean in first? Did Rook?

Who gave a damn?

She moved, or maybe he did, and their mouths met. The kiss was tender at first, questioning, her lips parted against his. Then she angled closer, opening for him, and Rook swept his tongue inside. He tasted like spice and smoke, wild and unfamiliar. Her hand slid up his chest, fingers curling into his shirt, holding on as if she might float away.

Something clattered to the floor, but she didn't care. All she knew was the way his lips moved against hers, hot and greedy and reverent. He kissed her like his life depended on it, and she felt exactly the same. Sasha had been kissed before, but never like that. She had never felt so seen, so saturated in a moment, so absolutely lifted out of her own skin.

Rook pulled back, his body as taut as a wire. The dim lantern light left his expression unreadable.

Sasha searched for something to say. So they kissed. So what? But her mouth couldn't form the words, not with the taste of him branded on her tongue.

"This cannot happen," Rook said. The words

were so final they felt like blows. "I have a duty here. I cannot be … distracted."

A distraction.

Sasha straightened and fought the scowl on her face. Was that all she was? A distraction? Some girl her ex could cheat on? Just no one.

She stood. "I don't think you're going to die. We should be safe here for tonight."

And in the morning, she would send him on his way and find a way to escape this insanity.

She wouldn't want to distract him any more than she already had.

7

SASHA WOKE in the old ranger's cabin.

For a suspended second, she didn't know where she was. The air inside the cracked little cabin was cool and thick with dust, faintly scented with old pine and whatever had lived in the walls. She could hear her own breath, uneven and shallow, caught somewhere between a gasp and a complaint.

It wasn't a nightmare.

Her hands curled in the scratchy wool of the blanket she had rescued from the back of a closet, one with too many stains to name and a few suspect holes chewed straight through. It barely kept the chill away. Not that she was cold. No, she was burning hot all over again as everything came roaring back.

Oh god, Erik was dead.

The memory slammed into her, visceral and so much more real now that the adrenaline was gone. There had been flames. Screaming. Hers and his. The blue-hot burst that had erased him. No body, no anything, just that last, hideous shape caught mid-turn. Her stomach clenched, and her throat closed against a scream. She pressed a hand flat to the bare floorboards, grounding herself as her pulse thudded in her ears.

She tried to breathe, tried to be present, tried to move. When she finally sat up with a sharp, awkward motion that left a twinge in her lower back, she realized she wasn't alone. The blanket slid off her shoulder in a slow, reluctant fall.

Rook was watching her.

He sat at the end of the table, the one with a gouged star carved into its edge. He wasn't slouched or sprawled. There was nothing loose or relaxed about the way he held himself, not even in a place as bleak and battered as this. Rook sat like he belonged on a marble throne, like he had spent the night keeping guard because it was his duty. One arm draped across his thigh, the other resting on the table, fingers splayed as if to anchor himself in place.

He looked like something swept in from a myth, dropped into a scene that didn't deserve him. A man out of time. If you stripped away the battered black shirt clinging to his frame and gave him a red cloak, he could have been a Roman general brooding over a war map. Or a medieval king, armored in chainmail and rage, waiting for news from the front.

Not someone in the middle of the California woods with sap on his boots, who kissed like he lived for it.

A faint band of sunrise squeezed through the greasy window, catching the rough edges of his jaw and the shadowed hollows under his eyes. He still looked powerful, still other, with an exhaustion so deep in his bones it gave her a strange ache in her chest.

But she was not going to think about the kiss. That way was madness.

Rook didn't want to kiss her again.

He had made it clear. Duty, distraction, all the things that belonged in books about tragic kings. Not in her cabin, not in her life. Sasha did not do tragic, and she was definitely not going to get involved with a guy who said he was a dragon and hunting alien slavers in her woods.

She needed to get home, shower the dirt and trauma off her skin, and forget all of this.

But even as she told herself that, another part of

her, a stubborn and traitorous echo of hope, lingered on that moment from last night. The heat of his mouth, the taste of him, the way his hand had felt on the back of her neck, both gentle and hungry.

She'd never been kissed like that. Not by Erik, or Andy before him, or any of the men she had tried to convince herself meant something. Not one of them had made her blood thrum the way Rook's hand in her hair had.

It was everything she had read about but never believed, a current that rewrote the rules of her body. It made her ache, made her angry, made her want.

Wanting him was the worst possible thing she could do.

She scrubbed her hands across her face and busied herself with pulling on her boots, knotting the laces tight as if to punish her wandering thoughts. Focus. Get up, gear up, survive.

"Good morning," she forced out. Her voice sounded scraped raw. She cleared her throat. "How's your shoulder?"

"Functional." Rook's answer was brief, almost clipped. His gaze flickered from her to the slatted window. His jaw tightened, every muscle going alert. "Stay there," he commanded. His voice was quiet but so final she almost obeyed.

He might have looked like a Roman general, but that didn't make Sasha his legionnaire. She untangled herself from the blanket, her feet finding the splintery boards with a caution bred by years of sneaking out of places she should not have been.

The moth-eaten curtain was drawn mostly over the window. Rook stood tense and tried to peer through a sliver of the glass. His hand hovered near the table's edge, his body drawn taut as a bowstring.

"Your fugitives?" she barely breathed. The words felt like prying open a door in her chest she desperately wanted to keep shut. They shouldn't have been able to find them there, not unless they were using some ultra-futuristic alien tech. The cabin was not on any recent maps. It was a spot passed down from trail guide to trail guide, a local secret.

Alien slavers need not apply.

Sasha edged to the other side of the window and lifted a corner of the curtain. Cold air trickled in, raising goosebumps along her arms. Through the grimy glass, she could make out big, shaggy shapes moving outside. One of the shapes lumbered up to the porch steps, sniffed a bit of old tarp, then rolled onto its back like it owned the place.

Relief unfurled inside her. Not total, but enough to unclench her shoulders.

"I will take care of this," Rook said, his voice low and dangerous as he rose to his feet.

Sasha's hand shot out. "What's there to take care of?"

"There are foul beasts stalking our camp," he announced, his voice fierce with alarm. His frame seemed to expand in the small room, his chest rising as if preparing for battle.

"Those are black bears." A sound that was half a laugh and half an exasperated sigh escaped her. "We're in *their* woods. And they won't try to come inside." She risked a look at him, her head tilted, and tried not to smile at the confusion on his face. "There's no food out. They won't bother us."

Her stomach chose that moment to protest, letting out a growl so loud that even Rook's eyebrows lifted a fraction. For a moment, the night's danger seemed absurd. Alien slavers were one thing, but California's oldest, laziest residents were just going about their morning, unbothered by dragons or women with yesterday's makeup smudged under their eyes.

Yet Rook stood rigid, prepared to face a monster. It took her a second to notice the faint wisp of what looked like actual smoke rising from his skin just above his collar. It shimmered in the weak light, coiling off him in barely visible threads.

"Are you smoking? How?" The words slipped free before she could catch them. She had seen impossible things in these woods. That still topped the list.

Rook glanced down at his arm as if surprised. "It does not matter. If you say they will leave, I shall trust you."

There was a moment, a kind of standoff, where she expected him to charge out there anyway, fire in his hands. Instead, he hesitated, his gaze searching her face before backing slowly away from the window. He moved with that same odd nobility, like a general making a calculated retreat. He stood a few feet back, arms folded over his chest, the strange smoke still curling gently from his skin.

Sasha kept her spot at the window. Outside, the bears wandered off, their heavy bodies disappearing into the trees. Their bulk and steadiness felt different from anything she had spent the night running from. Bears did not worry about dragon slayers or dead exes. Their world was food and sun and the gentle rhythm of the seasons.

It must be nice.

Her chest went tight with longing. Not for their

ease, she wasn't built for sleeping all winter, but for the simplicity of being. The simplicity of existing without the weight of everything trying to chase her out of the world.

For a moment, she watched the empty porch as if she could absorb its peace. The day outside carried on with or without her.

Behind her, Rook finally let out a breath. She didn't turn. She let herself wish for that kind of peace, even as she knew she would never have it. Not there. Not anywhere a man could set the woods on fire with a snap of his fingers.

Sasha pulled the curtain shut and stepped back from the window. She looked for coffee, or tea, or even an old can of beans. Anything that would taste like being alive and not hunted. For a while longer, she would let Rook think she was in control, that everything really would be all right. Because somebody had to be.

8

ROOK TRIED NOT to stare at Sasha as she led him down the narrow trail. The light snagged in her hair, finding the hidden strands of amber and auburn beneath the chestnut, painting her skin in delicate, golden strokes. She moved with a purpose that never left him behind, a half-step ahead, always aware of his injured shoulder.

She was a beauty. A temptation.

Forbidden.

Not by any law. Not by his king. But by his own code. Rook was on Earth for a job, to hunt down slavers and mete out his people's justice. He couldn't be sidetracked by soft hair and bright eyes.

Or softer lips.

His body remembered too much. Her warmth,

the taste of her, the way she'd melted against his mouth in that ruined cabin.

A mistake.

He'd told himself that a hundred times as morning crept through the grimy window. He was not there to take a mate, not there to court a human woman who looked at him like she wanted to discover the man beneath his battered armor and fire. He remembered his duty. He would not falter again.

Then she laughed, a joke tossed over her shoulder about a terrifying Yelp review, whatever that was, and Rook's focus shattered. He nearly tripped on a half-buried root, his boot catching just in time. He dug his heel into the pine needle duff as a sharp throb of warning shot through his bad arm.

Sasha's head jerked back, her ponytail swinging. She pinned him with an odd look. Not alarm. Not amusement. It was part curiosity, part worry, a complicated flicker in her pale green eyes.

"You all right there?"

"I am fine." The words came out short, fussy even to his own ears. He was annoyed with himself for being so easily caught off guard.

He couldn't risk losing his edge. There was no sign of the fugitives. He and Sasha had given his campsite a wide berth, but he could feel the minutes ticking by, the opportunity for justice narrowing with every step that took him farther from the hunt.

His mission hadn't changed. Track them down. Capture them for Vemion if he could. Incinerate them if he had to. But Sasha had to be clear of it. Safe. The tangled urge to shield her from harm had dug itself deep inside his chest and refused to let go. He'd already asked too much of her.

They fell into a companionable quiet, the hush of the forest broken only by the crunch of their boots and the occasional cry of a bird high in the pines.

After a while, Sasha paused, tilting her head as if listening to something only she could hear. She motioned for him to stop and pointed through the dense trees. Rook followed her gaze, confused, but then full of wonder. Two young deer picked their way through the ferns, their mother keeping watch just behind. The animals were elegant, so fragile looking he feared a single breath might spook them. Sasha didn't move, just smiled, her face open and almost childlike in the dappled light.

The deer vanished in a blink, melting into the green and gold. But the moment stuck with him. No dragon fire, not even the grandeur of the royal gardens back home, felt quite like that.

The wildness, the peace. He looked at Sasha,

puzzling over what kept her tied to a world so simple and vulnerable, yet so fiercely alive. The woods asked nothing of him but demanded everything. They were unforgiving, yet they gave her solace. He saw it in the easy set of her shoulders, the relaxed smile that lingered on her lips.

He didn't ask what it meant to her.

The day grew brighter, the world shifting from sleepy indigo to sharp, awakening green. Another hour passed. One foot, then the next. The woods started to look familiar, even to his eyes. The trees parted in ways he recognized, the undergrowth pressed flat by boot prints, new and old.

"Where are we?" he finally asked.

"Almost back to camp," she said, glancing over her shoulder. "More importantly, almost back to the parking lot where my van is."

Her voice was light, but her hand toyed with the strap of her backpack, twisting it, letting it fall.

"You're leaving?" The question escaped before he could stop it. He tried to keep his tone flat, disinterested. That was the plan. He needed her safe. So why did the words feel like a betrayal?

She stopped walking and scuffed her boot in the duff. "I'm not fit to handle fire-breathing dragons from outer space." She gave him a crooked, strained smile. "There are maps in the supply tent that will help. Unless you want me to stick around and be your guide ..." She trailed off, the invitation hanging in the air between them. He saw hope in her eyes, but it was tangled with worry, maybe even fear.

He didn't know what to say. The words were stuck in his throat.

They stood in an awkward silence, both pretending to study the fallen needles at their feet. Their eyes met for a second, then darted away. He refused to ask her to stay. She was right. It was too dangerous, and he couldn't let her get hurt. The need to keep her safe had become a chasm inside him, an absolute truth that defied all logic.

Finally, he forced out the words he owed her. "Thank you." They felt as heavy as stones. "I may not have survived last night without you."

Sasha's smile was tired but real. "I'd ask you to leave a good review, but this isn't the kind of thing that anyone would believe."

The trees thinned ahead, revealing sparser brush. Sasha pointed. "The parking lot is right through there." She hesitated, her hand hovering near her hip as if she wanted to reach out but couldn't. "It's just ... never mind."

"What?" The question sounded raw, more demanding than he intended.

She fiddled with the sleeve of her flannel, gathering her courage. Her cheeks flushed a faint pink against the green of the woods. "Can I see you do the fire thing? One last time?" The words came out in a rush, as if she was afraid they'd get stuck. "I mean, I know it's probably nothing to you, but ..." She shrugged, looking anywhere but at him.

He couldn't have said no if his life depended on it.

"Of course," he answered, his voice quiet but certain.

He summoned the flame, letting a single ember coil to life above his palm. Then, for her, he called up more. The fire burned hotter, brighter, swirling upward in a ribbon of living gold. He shed all his restraint, guiding the blaze into shapes she would know. A twisting helix. A burst of heat. The glow reflected in her eyes, turning them a wild, impossible green.

His instructors would have chastised him for wasting power on spectacle. Fire was a weapon, not a toy. But he wanted to show off for her. He needed to see that light in her tired face. The pull toward her, impossible and magnetic, overruled everything.

When his energy began to dip, he gently closed his fist, and the fire dissolved into a shimmer of heat between them.

Sasha just stood there, eyes wide, a real smile blooming on her face. "That was amazing. Thank you."

She hesitated, her gaze searching his. Then, before he could move, she closed the small distance between them.

Her hand rose to cup his cheek, her touch warm and sure. Her thumb feathered just beneath his eye, and a jolt went through him, pure and clean. She leaned in and brushed her lips softly against his.

It was a fleeting, gentle kiss that held no questions, only a farewell. It was light as a breath, and it hollowed him out more completely than the raw, messy clash in the cabin. This was tender. Final. A goodbye pressed into his skin.

She stepped back, her hand dropping. Her eyes were shining with a storm of feeling. Longing, regret, and something that looked a lot like hope she was trying to stomp flat.

"Goodbye, Rook."

She turned, squared her shoulders, and walked away. Her boots crunched over gravel as she headed toward the brightening edge of the woods. With every step she took, the strange ache inside him grew, as if something vital, something that belonged to him, was being torn away.

9

ROOK WASN'T JUST GOING to leave Sasha alone.

He didn't tell her he followed, but he did. The old hunter's urge, part duty and part something hungrier, drove him. His steps made no sound. He stayed just far enough back, concealed behind a tangle of young fir, then a veil of ferns.

She crossed from dirt to the ragged bite of gravel, then to the rutted pavement of the small parking lot. A large, battered brown van was one of two vehicles parked there. The other probably belonged to the human the slavers had killed. He watched her lift her chin, scanning the empty lot with a wariness he recognized. She checked every shadow before moving, her eyes narrowed against the morning sun.

This would be the perfect place for an ambush.

The jagged edge of the forest pressed against the

crumbled curb. Too many places for a man to hide. He could see it all: the narrow lane in, the choke points, the way a pair of dragons with their fire primed could sweep the lot before she reached the van. He cursed himself for ever letting her walk alone.

He summoned his fire and waited.

Everything in him went sharp, his senses stretching wide. The distant wail of a bird overhead spiked the hair along his arms. He scanned the reflection in the van's windows. Was that movement inside? A slaver's eye, waiting? The bitter taste of anticipation curled on his tongue.

Tension threaded through his limbs. He watched for the flicker of a shadow, for a glint of metal or flame. The air felt too bright, as if the world was holding its breath for violence.

Sasha snapped the van door open. She ducked in fast, tossed her backpack onto the passenger seat, and slammed herself behind the wheel. For half a second, Rook braced for glass to shatter, for fire to slice through metal. He closed one fist, flame tingling at his fingertips, ready to burn anyone who showed themselves.

The engine coughed and sputtered, hacking like an old man, then caught with a shudder. Its rattle filled the lot. Tires crunched over gravel as she reversed.

Rook waited for an attack. His pulse thundered. He scanned for any ripple in the brush, any excuse to scorch the earth bare. His gaze darted between the woods, the trash bin, and the cracked public toilet. All perfect cover.

But nothing materialized. No movement, no sudden flare of fire. Only the wind hissing in the needles and the rumbling complaint of the van as Sasha straightened it out and drove away.

He remained a shadow, blending into the tree line long after she'd turned south and disappeared from sight. Only when the last faint cough of the engine faded did the tension in his shoulders ease.

The dragon inside him snarled, pressing at the cage of his flesh. He wanted to break free. He wanted to shift, to scream out a challenge, his wings tearing through the new day's light. He wanted to hunt above the treetops, to see for miles and be certain her path was safe and clear.

The urge was so strong his fingers curled, digging half-moons into his palms.

He shouldn't have let her go. The wild, primitive knowledge burned through him. Only he could keep her safe. She was his to protect. His responsibility.

She was ... his. The word was sharp, possessive, and undeniable.

He was going mad.

A dry wind caught his face, prickling along his jaw. The emptiness the van left behind was louder than its engine. He was a lord of Vemion and felt like an abandoned cub pining for the warmth of a den.

He vaguely recalled something Shade, the Royal Matchmaker, had said to him. He'd dismissed her words at the time, but they ran through his mind with a sharp clarity now.

Your mate will drive you mad.

If some human on a backwater planet could make him feel this way, he shuddered to think what his dragon-mate would make him feel. He hoped he never met her. The thought was terrifying.

He forced himself to melt deeper into the trees, pulling away from the clearing. Away from him, there was no reason for the fugitives to chase her. She was just one person among billions. She would be safe.

Even if it didn't feel that way.

He turned and headed back toward the ranger station. The fugitives had found his camp, but they hadn't yet found his ship. It was shielded, cloaked so that scanning tech from Vemion would struggle to pick it out. Still, he didn't want to risk going back there now. A single careless move could expose everything.

He needed to talk to someone, he realized. To get his head on straight. He was too far into his own thoughts, last night's tension knotting his insides. And there was only one group of people in this galaxy stubborn enough to give him advice he might actually heed: his brothers, Vex and Zane.

As the eldest, Rook hated to admit he might need advice. He'd always been the one to issue orders and take the blows first. But he wasn't fool enough to put it off any longer.

He found a sheltered hollow among a ring of huge pines. With careful hands, he drew out his communicator and set it on the ground. It glimmered with faint blue light, reading his signature. He initiated the call. After several moments, the air flickered with static that resolved into two figures before him, ghostly but vivid.

Zane was the first to move, arms folded insolently across his chest. Wild dark hair fell in a rakish swoop over one eye, his smirk quick and sharp. Vex stood a half-head taller, his bearing as strict as a royal guard. Where Zane vibrated with restless energy, Vex was all iron restraint.

Zane gave an exaggerated look around, his mouth making a long O as he surveyed Rook's surroundings. "This doesn't look like Rook's cruiser, does it, Vex?"

Vex furrowed his brow, scanning the moss and sagging pine behind Rook. "I can't say it does. If I'm not mistaken, those are the forests of Earth."

Rook suppressed a snarl.

Zane rocked back on his heels, grinning. "I always pictured your exile would be on some desert moon, not a mud pit."

Vex's lips twitched. "Have you finished the mission, or did you just want to chat?"

Rook's jaw ticked. He had little patience for games. "Fine, yes," he relented. "Your help may have been appreciated. The situation is more complex than anticipated."

Zane snorted. "You mean the fugitives didn't fall to the ground in fear once they saw you?"

"They did not," Rook said, his tone flat.

"And they fought back when you attempted to use your fire against them?" That was from Vex. "Yes."

"Injured you?" Vex's eyes narrowed on his left shoulder as if he could see beneath the battered shirt.

How did they always know? He straightened,

shifting his posture to hold his left shoulder back. The healing salve had worked. It barely twinged.

"You need us," Zane said lightly, stretching his arms overhead.

"I can handle this myself." He clenched his fists. This was a mistake.

Zane leaned closer, peering at Rook. "Yes, going to Earth alone was a mistake," he snapped back. "Which is why we asked you to wait two days for us to be ready to travel. But no, the mighty Lord Rook needs to do it all himself." He rolled his eyes.

"That's enough," Rook snapped.

"Do you want us to come help clean up your mess?" Zane raised an eyebrow.

"No." He would eat glass before he asked for help.

"Then I don't know why you're calling. I'll see you at your funeral." Zane's figure blinked out, leaving Rook alone with Vex.

A heavy silence settled.

"He's in a mood," Rook offered.

Vex pursed his lips, his arms crossed. "You acted rashly in going there alone. It's unlike you. Why?" His gaze was a scalpel.

He wasn't going to tell Vex about his meeting

with the Royal Matchmaker, about Shade and her schemes. He'd never hear the end of it.

"I am doing my job," he said after a long pause. "And I need to return to it."

Vex didn't press. His tone softened a fraction. "Don't get killed, brother," he said quietly.

Then he, too, faded out, the hologram collapsing into empty air. The woods felt too silent.

Rook sat back on a rock and groaned, pressing his knuckles into his knees.

Don't get killed.

Easy to say.

All he had to do was find the fugitives, capture them, and return to Vemion, leaving Earth behind for good.

And never seeing Sasha again.

10

VAN LIFE LOOKED COOLER on TikTok.

Sasha hissed as her elbow slammed against the tiny counter that served as her kitchen, office, and dining room. She glared at the dented aluminum, rubbing the tender spot.

"Just great." She wrenched open a sticky cabinet and fished out a stale granola bar, her third of the day. Eight months ago, the choice had seemed brilliant. Move in with three nightmare roommates or put her meager savings into sprucing up a van as old as she was.

The thrill of freedom and open highways had called to her. She'd told herself she was minimalist enough, frugal enough, independent enough.

Now she just missed her stuff. Her battered French press. The stack of paperback novels she'd hauled through five states. Socks that didn't vanish into the void.

"Don't worry about that," Sasha said, her voice sharp. She focused on the small, familiar annoyances to avoid the bigger problem. To avoid thinking about who she'd left behind.

Rook.

Pain twisted in her chest. She told herself she wasn't thinking about him, but her traitorous brain summoned him with every hot draft through the window, with every flicker of red-gold sunlight that reminded her of a dragon's fire.

She definitely *was* thinking about him.

It had been two days. Not a word. No weird phone calls, no tall, broad-shouldered men with golden eyes knocking on her window, not even a note taped to the windshield. Nothing. The world trudged along as if it hadn't split wide open to reveal that fire breathing monsters were very real.

The slavers hadn't appeared. She scanned every shadow, every passing stranger, half expecting one of them to step out from behind the laundromat. Nothing. The campers at Rugged Trails Motorhome Lodge showed no signs of alarm.

Yesterday, the tour group that was due back radioed that the lower trail was flooded, so they were detouring and would be delayed another day. On paper, everything was normal.

Except now she knew what normal was hiding. Now she knew about dragons and aliens, and everything real felt dangerously fake.

She'd only known him for a few hours, yet it felt like she'd left a piece of herself with him in that forest. A wild, reckless piece she'd tried so hard to outgrow.

She flopped face down on the van's tiny bed, clutching the pillow. "I need to get laid," she grumbled into the mattress.

The thought was a lie, and her body knew it. It only brought her back to the kiss. The memory of it in the ruined cabin, Rook's mouth hot and seeking on hers, his hands trembling where they gripped her waist. That kiss had felt like it could have been the beginning of something. Something reckless, world-ending. New. Then she remembered his fire display, the ribbon of gold and red that had danced in the air just for her.

And the second kiss, a goodbye that had stung more than she could have imagined.

Sitting in her van wasn't helping, clearly.

Sasha swung her legs off the bed, pulled on her boots, and got out to stretch. She was parked in her usual spot, a patch of gravel at the back of a row of battered RVs. In the late afternoon, the place was alive with the bustle of arrival and return. Engines rumbled. Folding chairs scraped open. A neighbor's barbecue sent the sharp smell of burning onions into the air.

She walked through it all, her body alive with nervous energy. Every shout made her jump. She scanned for alien eyes, for hard jawlines, for signs of anything otherworldly.

But there was only the familiar litany of RV life. Hoses coiled beneath bumpers, dogs yapping, someone grumbling about a leak.

"Hey, girl, thought you'd finally pulled out for greener pastures." The voice was raspy with too many cigarettes and too much laughter.

Sasha turned and smiled automatically. Janice stood there in a faded tie-dyed shirt and cargo shorts, a battered straw hat on her cropped gray hair. She clutched a beer can, her rings catching flashes of sunlight. "I'd say goodbye if I did," Sasha promised.

"That makes one of you, honey." Janice's eyes lingered on Sasha's face, sharp and knowing. "People come, people go."

Sasha willed herself not to flinch. The words brought Erik's face flashing to mind.

Someone had to have noticed he was missing by now. No cops had come by asking questions, but they would. And what the hell would she tell them? Alien dragons burnt him to a crisp when they decided they didn't want to leave witnesses?

If she thought her van was tiny, she didn't want to find out how cramped a padded cell was.

"Who left?" she asked, pushing the thought away.

"Vanessa, over in one of the rentals. Little nurse, cute nose ring. I've been poking around, but nobody's seen her in days."

"Oh." Sasha knew Vanessa a little. "Last I heard, she was talking about getting an apartment."

Janice sniffed, unconvinced. "Could be, but she left her cactus on the windowsill, and that plant was her baby." She shrugged, finishing her beer with a practiced swig. "But what do I know?" With a wave, Janice wandered off.

Sasha drifted along the cracked road, her boots scuffing the gravel. The air smelled like hot dust, pine needles, and sunscreen. It was all so fucking ordinary.

She read the community board outside the shower block out of habit. Flyers for dog sitters and yoga classes blurred past until her eyes snagged on the word MISSING.

Vanessa's smiling face stared back at her from an off-center selfie.

Have you seen this person?

The flyer listed her description, her car, and a phone number to call. So Janice was right. Vanessa hadn't just left.

Then Sasha noticed the other posters. More of them lined the board now. A man with a sheepish smile under a fisherman's cap. Two kids in matching hoodies. A young woman named Monica whom Sasha sometimes saw doing her laundry late at night.

What had Rook said again? The slavers came to Earth to take people. Had Erik been helping them find victims? People no one would miss. Except they were missed. Missed enough for these faded, hopeful posters.

Her stomach tightened. She had to find Rook. She had to figure this out. But how was she supposed to call down an alien dragon lord? She didn't exactly have his number.

Sasha cursed, shoving her hands through her hair.

She felt it first. A wave of heat, unnatural against

the fading warmth of the day. The hairs on her arms prickled. A thunderous crack shattered the air before she could process it. The explosion rattled up her spine, and a dark plume of smoke unspooled from the north end of the park. Another bang followed, closer this time, and the world tipped into chaos.

People ran, screaming, their faces blank with panic. Sasha stood frozen, her mind scrambling for a rational explanation.

A gas leak. A generator accident.

Her hope died when a man strode onto the main path—one of the slavers. Even at this distance, the dark, metallic glint of his bodysuit caught the setting sun. He moved with an unnatural confidence, a weapon from a nightmare cradled in his hands. It had a glowing red barrel and wires coiling around the grip.

Her body finally remembered how to move. She bolted, her boots hammering the dry ground as she dove behind a nearby dumpster.

Two more slavers emerged, their strange weapons sweeping side to side. They fired in short bursts that sent fountains of dirt into the air. One blast caught a folding table, which erupted in an unnatural blue fire.

Sasha hunched lower. Running for her van was a death sentence. She couldn't outrun that fire.

A sob scraped through the noise. Janice was down near the laundry block, clutching a bloody thigh, her face pale with shock.

Sasha's heart hammered. She dropped to a crouch and darted across the open space. "I got you," she hissed, skidding to Janice's side.

"Shot me," Janice gasped. Sasha hooked her arms under Janice's and dragged her behind a toppled recycling bin, gritting her teeth against the weight. She pressed a hand to the wound, her fingers coming away slick with blood and fear.

"Stay with me," she whispered.

A slaver stalked past their hiding spot, his weapon held loosely, his eyes scanning the campsites. Was he looking for her? Or was she just unlucky? In the end, it didn't matter.

There was no running from this. Not anymore. She could hide, or she could fight.

If she was going to survive, she had to fight.

11

ROOK TRACKED the energy signature through a tangle of blackened trees. His boots snapped twigs and kicked up ash that stuck to his sweaty face. When he emerged at the edge of the forest, he found a world unraveling in fire.

Night had barely fallen, but the sky rippled with unnatural red light. Sparks leaped ten feet from burning tents, and flames writhed in angry rings through the campsites. People's screams mixed with the undercurrent of slaver voices barking in a clipped, sharp-edged tongue.

Explosions erupted between the vehicles, rocking the rows of battered campers and sending shrapnel into the weeds. The air reeked of burning fuel and something sweeter that made his stomach turn. Burned flesh had a smell you didn't forget.

He caught their shapes through the flickering light. A cluster of terrified humans huddled with their hands raised, herded by two slavers in armor. Their eyes glowed like lanterns in the smoky dark.

A fifteen-foot wall of living fire flickered between the hostages and the forest, penning them in a circle of pure terror. Every time one of them tried to cross that boundary, the flames licked higher with a warning hiss. The cries of the trapped pushed against his skull. Someone shouted a name. Someone else sobbed, their lungs scorched raw. The slavers didn't care. Their attention was fixed outward, scanning for new victims.

He should have known this was coming.

The silence of the last two days had been too thick. He'd crashed through ravines, snagging his pants on thorns and nearly twisting his ankle three times while chasing erratic bursts of energy on his battered tracker. Every trail ended at a blank telepad or a deliberately set fire.

Now, with grim clarity, he saw the truth. The slavers had been running him in circles like an idiot, laying a false trail while they plotted to gather their prey.

He wanted to burn this whole rotten place down to the roots. Rook dropped to a half-crouch, letting the scent of burning pine fill his nose and the heat soak into his skin. He spotted the telltale black of a slaver's uniform up the main road, striding toward two cowering children pressed against the bumper of a rusted-out trailer.

There was no time to think.

He lunged. Fire rolled from his hand, a ribbon of molten orange that tore through the sagging under-brush. The slaver didn't even see him coming, didn't see him for what he was: a dragon lord, not some Earth stray. The fire hit center mass and folded the slaver's armor like cheap fabric, toppling him into the dirt. The force of it shook the ground, a tremor that sent one of the human children sliding backward.

Too close. The boy screamed, his hair singed where the flame had shot past. Shit. Fury slammed through Rook. If his focus slipped, if his fire was a degree off, these people would die just as surely as by slaver hands.

He closed his fist, squeezing the fire back into his veins until it snarled and bucked inside him.

Gods, he hated this planet.

He hated that his fire was the only thing he had, and sometimes it was too much. He couldn't arm himself with the weapons the humans used, primi-tive, reckless things that were loud and unpredictable. A blaster might have been practical, but he was a dragon. This was a matter of pride, of blood. The ancient Vemion code settled heavy in his bones. His fire was his honor, his birthright, and, right now, his curse.

He surged forward, pushing past the fallen slaver. The child and his sister broke free, running flat-out down a gap between two vans.

He pressed deeper into the heart of the camp. The slavers were everywhere, but for all their strength, they were distracted. The humans had finally begun to fight back. In a clearing, a trio of men crouched behind an overturned picnic table, wielding hunting rifles and garden tools. Someone swung a cast-iron skillet at a slaver, the clang cutting through the air. The slavers had their attention split, and it was costing them.

He nearly tripped on a cooler as he looped around a grove of pines, heat beating at his face from a tent that was completely engulfed in flames. That was when he saw her.

Tucked behind a battered brown van, a model so familiar it made his stomach drop, a woman fought like the world wouldn't wait for her to figure things out: Sasha.

She was surrounded by a half-dozen humans: an

older woman clutching a bloody rag to her leg, a whip-thin boy wielding a hedge trimmer with shaking hands, a man in a plaid shirt bleeding from a scalp wound that had matted half his hair. They'd dragged recycling bins and broken chairs into a rough barricade that wouldn't have stopped a determined raccoon, let alone alien slavers.

Sasha held a huge red canister in her hands. She hefted it like a weapon, her shoulders straining under the weight. As a slaver raised his palm, Sasha pointed the black tube coming out of the top of the canister and squeezed. White, choking foam blasted out, smothering the flames as they leaped from the slaver's hand. The jet soaked his boots and knocked him off-balance.

Pride rushed through him. Sasha's eyes blazed with determination. She shouted instructions to her little band, telling the boy when to duck and when to reload her pistol. Every time a slaver drew near, Sasha stood in front, brave and stupid all at once.

She was going to get herself killed.

He absorbed every detail in a single heartbeat. They barely knew each other. She should mean nothing to him. Yet he felt branded by the sight of her, shouting, sweating, reckless, stubborn, and so utterly alive.

She fought like someone who knew losing wasn't an option.

Sasha fell back as the humans with guns began firing. The volley was deafening. Rook recoiled from the sound of the human weapons. They were crude, all thunder and hot-iron stench that made his nose burn. It was a miracle anyone had survived long enough to use them.

And yet, the slaver closest to the fort jerked backward, clutching his side where bullets found the gap in his armor. He fell, blood spilling onto the dirt, and didn't rise again.

All right, Rook conceded. Earth weapons had their uses.

Their victory was short-lived. A pair of slavers flanked the barricade, slipping in behind a burning RV. Sasha, focused on foaming down another blade of fire, backed right into the open. She was unaware that new threats were closing in.

Everything in him went bright and sharp. He didn't think. He didn't strategize. He just roared an old war cry and let his fire fly. The jet caught the slavers square in their chests. They staggered, howling as flames crawled up their torsos. For a split second, it was glorious.

Then Sasha, hearing him, stepped toward the jet of fire.

His heart plummeted. He tried to pull the fire back, but it was too late. There was no calling it home. He was about to watch her burn—the woman who had stubbornly marched into his thoughts, who had kissed him, who had awakened things in him he'd sworn to keep buried.

His voice broke through the chaos, a single word ripped from his throat. "No!"

Sasha's head snapped around, her eyes locking onto his. Maybe she read everything in his face, because she lifted both hands as if to brace herself. The fire crashed over her, wild and searing.

And did nothing.

The flames split around her like water against stone, coiling harmlessly over her hair and skin. She blinked as the heat whipped her hair back, but she didn't flinch. She stood untouched, the impossible surrounding her.

He stared, everything going silent except for the high whine of disbelief in his skull. No ordinary human on any world survived the direct burn of a dragon lord's fire. Only one kind of person could do that.

His mate.

He'd heard the stories of other dragons who fell for human women, whose flames marked them out as special.

He hadn't truly believed it.

He wanted to sink to his knees in the middle of this burning chaos and take her face in his hands, but there was no time for fated revelations; the fight wasn't over.

He stormed across the campground, letting his fire rip. He didn't care anymore if the humans watched, didn't care if everyone in this town woke up wondering why a man wielded fire in his palms.

Sasha was there. He would raze the world before he let her die.

She spotted him at twenty paces and grinned as if she'd conjured him from the night itself.

"Nice of you to show up!" she shouted, her voice scratchy but defiant. Her hair was singed at the ends, and she had a nasty cut above her eye.

"I got tired of sitting in the woods," he shot back, his gaze locking on hers. Deep inside, something unspooled, tension draining from him as if her presence burned through his fear.

Sasha ducked a fireball and tossed him the empty canister. "Make yourself useful, Dragon Lord. I'm out of foam, and my deodorant gave up an hour ago."

He caught it, the foam residue cold and sticky on his palms. He tossed it aside. No need for tools now. He swept another wall of fire across the camp, cutting off three slavers trying to circle the fort. The humans huddled tighter, watching him in awe and terror and maybe a spark of hope.

"Is that your friend?" the older woman called out, pulling a kid behind cover.

Sasha nodded, her smile wild. "He's on our side!"

Together, they fought their way through the burning maze. Rook shielded Sasha, his fire driving slavers back while the small band of human fighters covered their escape. His shirt stuck to his back with sweat, and his throat burned from the smoke.

But no matter how hard they fought, it wasn't enough. The slavers fell back, regrouping at the northern edge with three fresh prisoners. He watched, helpless, as a grenade burst into white light. When the smoke cleared, the slavers and their captives were gone.

He caught Sasha's eye, saw the frustration and exhaustion on her face. Red and blue lights swept the tree line. A mechanical wailing started in the distance, growing louder, more insistent.

"What's that?" he asked, keeping one eye on the edge of the camp.

"That's the cavalry. The cops," she clarified, catching his confusion. "Someone reported all the gunfire and actual fire. They're going to want to know what's going on." She was already shoving the wounded forward, barking orders. Then her eyes cut to his. "You should probably get out of here. They'll have a lot of questions, and 'I'm a dragon from space' isn't going to go over well on the incident report."

He hesitated. He'd never abandon a fight, but he recognized the hard line of her jaw. She was right. He couldn't explain himself or his fire, not to these people.

He closed the small distance between them and took her hand. It was small, battered, and alive. He'd let her out of his sight once. He couldn't do it again.

"Come with me," he said, the words low and rough in his chest.

12

A SOB of relief nearly broke free. Adrenaline sweated out of every pore as she ran. She'd be an idiot not to follow Rook. If he asked her to leap off a cliff right now, she might just do it—her judgment was that shot.

They kept low, dodging a toppled trash can and sliding through the smoke-choked shadow between the bathhouse and her van. Rook moved like he'd been bred for this, all purpose and control, while her limbs felt like overcooked spaghetti. Her van crouched on the far edge of the lot, its battered brown sides splattered with ash and god-knows-what smudged on the windows. Its familiar ugliness was the only thing that made sense anymore.

Red and blue lights spun across the ruined lot.

The police, late as always, were wading into mayhem long after everything good was already on fire.

She jerked at Rook's sleeve, nearly missing when she spotted a box truck pulling out fast. It skidded over crushed cooler lids and half-melted tents, white and dented with one busted headlight and a long, wet streak of blood arced across the passenger door.

Her stomach dropped so hard she tasted bile. "They're taking people," she whispered, her voice like sandpaper. "Look."

Rook didn't speak, but his eyes flashed with something that definitely wasn't human. He gave one sharp nod.

No time for panic. No time for nonsense. Sasha ran for her van, keys already a fist of metal digging into her palm.

She skidded into the driver's seat, sweat making her shirt stick uncomfortably to her back, and Rook was beside her in an instant. He was too big for the cramped passenger side, his knees jammed against her grocery bag full of dirty clothes, his shoulders hunched so he wouldn't crack his head on the ceiling.

"Buckle up," she snapped, voice sharp with terror and a weird, giddy hope. "This is about to get bumpy." As if seatbelts would matter if the slavers decided to light them up.

The van's engine coughed like an old man with smoker's lungs but caught. Sasha muttered a quick prayer to every benevolent roadside god she'd ever scorned. "Not now, baby, I need you one more time."

By some miracle of unreliable machinery, the van lurched forward. Sasha jammed it into gear, swinging wide around a toppled picnic table. Her windshield was smeared with smoke and what might be bird poop from three days ago. She stole a split-second glance at her rearview mirror. Sirens flickered, chaos boiling beneath the hang of pine and fir.

Chasing monsters into the night. That was new.

She could taste adrenaline, metallic and hot in her mouth, mixing with the burn of old coffee and the sour-sweet tang of melted plastic drifting in through the cracked window. Rook's body heat made the already stuffy van feel like a sauna. Her T-shirt was glued to her lower back with sweat.

As soon as they cleared the lot and shot onto the two-lane road, tires squealing on loose gravel, it hit her all at once. She was alive. She should be dead but wasn't. Heady, wild relief warred with fresh panic.

That fire. Impossible, beautiful fire. She'd walked

straight through it and hadn't so much as singed a hair. How?

She caught Rook's eye, trying to read danger or guilt or maybe an answer in his face. But he watched the road ahead, jaw clenched tight enough to crack walnuts, his hands knotted in his lap.

She swallowed hard. "Why didn't the fire touch me?" Her voice cracked like thin ice.

He didn't answer, at least not right away. The van rattled and groaned as they took a corner fast enough to nearly throw her through the window. The box truck's taillights flickered ahead, weaving through the darkness just past the twitchy edge of her headlights.

Sasha's insides twisted. Fine. If he wouldn't talk, she would. Talking kept her from screaming.

"I watched Erik burn," she blurted out, words tumbling like rocks down a hill. "And then that fire was thrown at me, it was coming straight for me. I should be a pile of ash. But I'm not. I ..."

She bit her tongue hard enough to taste blood. Don't break, not now.

The van barreled up the winding road, the forest crowding close, her headlights stuttering between trunks and brush. Every so often, she almost lost the truck, but she pressed on, hands white-knuckled on the wheel.

Rook finally spoke, his voice so low she almost missed it beneath the engine's wheezing. "You are ... marked."

Marked? Her chest squeezed. Like a dog, or a tree, or a ...

She pushed out a shaky laugh that sounded more like a hiccup. "You want to maybe get a little less cryptic and a little more specific? Because when people from outer space burn down my backyard, I like my answers in full sentences."

His jaw flexed, a muscle jumping beneath his skin. "My fire cannot harm you," he said. "You are immune."

A beat passed, heavy as wet canvas. She flinched at the words, amazed and confused and scared down to her toes.

Her voice, when it came, was barely above a whisper. "Immune? Why?"

He stared at the dashboard like it had personally offended him. "It's ... rare."

Great. Fan-freaking-tastic. "Rare how? Like, lucky-me rare, or you're-about-to-sacrifice-me-in-a-dragon-ritual rare?"

A faint tremor ran through him, anger or pain or

maybe something worse. He didn't answer, just pressed his hand to the dashboard. Smoke curled from his skin, briefly lighting the van's interior. The smell of burning plastic made her nose wrinkle.

Her left butt cheek had gone numb from sitting tense for so long. "You're not allowed to keep secrets if we're about to die, you know."

Rook's gaze finally landed on her, all hungry intensity and simmering heat. For one dangerous second, she wished he'd just say whatever it was, no matter how impossible. Even the crazy truth was better than the silence gnawing at her nerves.

She took the next corner sharper than she should, barely missing an old mailbox. "Don't you dare throw one of those fireballs in here," she said, aiming for cool but landing on desperate. "This thing's duct tape can handle a lot, but not alien pyrotechnics."

A ghost of a smile flickered on Rook's lips, the tension in him easing by a hair.

"No fire," he agreed.

Back to business. The box truck ahead swerved hard, its rear door bucking open an inch. It was just enough for Sasha to see two wide, terrified eyes peeking out before a rough hand yanked them back.

She almost choked. "People. They're still alive."

Her mind raced through an inventory of her van's contents. Road flares. First aid kit. A heavy Maglite with batteries that might be dead. Nothing that would help against space dragons.

She pressed the gas, the van roaring its complaint. "Hang on," she barked to Rook, her fingers slick with sweat as she yanked the wheel around another curve.

Action soothed her terror, gave her something to do besides feel every splinter in her soul. She focused on the road, the hunter, not the hunted. The headlights bounced, slicing through deep green and black, and she gritted her teeth, repeating silent pep talks with every slam of the suspension.

This wasn't supposed to be her life. She was the one who showed tourists how not to die when a bear got curious. Not alien slavers. Not dragon fire. Not this.

You're not running, you're fighting. Keep the wheel between you and the monsters.

A dry laugh threatened to escape. She swallowed it, jaw clenched.

"If we survive this," she said, "and you still insist on dodging basic questions, I'm leaving you in the woods with the next group of Instagram hikers. The ones who wear flip-flops on ten-mile hikes."

Beside her, Rook shifted, the van's door creaking under his bulk. He looked at her like she was the only thing not currently on fire. "I will explain," he said finally, the words like torn fabric, "later."

"Convenient," she snapped. "You save my life, they torch my ex like a piece of kindling, and now we're chasing bad guys in my rolling trash heap. And you still get to keep secrets?"

Rook's fingers hovered above hers on the gearshift. His heat soaked through, dangerously intimate. She needed to pee. Of all the stupid times for her bladder to chime in.

"Trust me," he said, softer now. "Please."

She almost shattered at that. All her walls, painfully built and loved and battered, wanted to tumble down. His plea took her by surprise. She didn't know what to do with it.

The van bounced over a pothole, nearly launching them through the roof. Sasha cursed, feeling a sharp pain shoot up her spine where she'd already bruised it during the fight back at camp.

"Don't die now, baby. If the aliens and the cops don't get us, your transmission might."

Another swerving flash of taillights caught her eye. The box truck was picking up speed, trying to shake them on the twisting descent toward the old service road. Sasha's gut coiled with dread. If they disappeared onto the fire road, she'd lose their trail. No, not happening.

She punched the gas and slammed into a lower gear, the familiar whine of overtaxed mechanics grinding beneath her. The van shuddered, threatened to give out, but she bullied it forward, bumping hard over a rut, her heart thundering so fiercely she felt dizzy.

A tremor worked through her as she mustered every scrap of courage she'd ever claimed. She risked a glance at Rook. His face looked all cut angles and shadow in the low light. He was battered, maybe even bleeding, but still a force of will. She could feel him watching her, measuring, weighing, wanting to speak.

Or wanting to bolt.

The truck's taillights vanished around a bend. Sasha jammed her foot down hard, reckless now. She refused to lose them.

He was silent, wrestling whatever truths warred inside him. His hand trembled once on his thigh, then stilled. The van jolted again, and her hand slipped off the gear stick, brushing his thigh. They both froze. Heat ripped up her arm, the taste of danger sweet and devastating.

Sasha exhaled a shaky breath, trying to steady herself before she came undone. She watched the road, winding faster, biting at the edge of what the ancient van could handle.

They sped past a roadside cross, then a sudden scatter of rocks, headlights flaring across the battered blue mailbox she'd always joked would spell her doom. Not tonight.

But her van was sputtering and heaving, and the higher they climbed, the less sure she was they'd make it anywhere.

13

ROOK WINCED as Sasha took a corner at high speed. The Earth vehicle didn't feel safe, and he was worried it might explode and take them with it before he could bring the slavers to justice.

At least he would die by his mate's side.

His *mate*.

He still couldn't quite believe it. But he'd seen it. He'd *felt* it. His fire had found her and had done her no harm.

The revelation crashed through him like a tidal wave, changing the landscape of everything he thought he knew. His chest felt too tight, his pulse throbbing in his temples. Since he'd left Vemion, he'd been certain of one thing: his mission.

Now that certainty had shattered, replaced by something wilder, more primal, more terrifying. Not the comfortable weight of duty, but this reckless, burning need to protect her, to claim her, to never let her out of his sight again.

He'd always expected to find his mate among his own kind. Not there. Not this stubborn, brave, impossibly fragile human woman with her ridiculous van and her inability to back down from a fight.

"Right?" Sasha was saying.

"Right," he agreed, without any idea of what she'd just said.

"You're telling me that little green men live in your engine and—fuck!" The vehicle jolted, and Rook pitched forward in his seat, forehead smacking against the dashboard. "Seatbelt!" Sasha yelled, too late.

The van gave a final, wheezing cough before the engine died completely. Steam hissed from under the hood, smelling of scorched metal and burning oil. The silence that followed was deafening after the constant rattle and groan of the dying engine. Something ticked, hot metal cooling in the night air. The headlights flickered once, twice, then plunged them into darkness.

"No, no, no," Sasha muttered, smacking the steering wheel with both palms. She twisted the key again and again. The engine made a grinding noise but refused to turn over. "Come on, you piece of garbage." She reached under the dash and fiddled with something, cursing under her breath. "They're fucking getting away, and you go and fail me now. I should have scrapped you months ago." She slammed her fist down on the console, and he heard a mechanical pop.

He didn't need to know Earth technology to know that that wasn't good.

"May I be of assistance?" he asked.

Sasha jabbed at the strap holding her in place until it released and shoved her car door open, not responding.

His mate had a temper.

Noted.

Mate. Mate. Mate. The word kept echoing in his head. He had more important things to think about. The slavers had taken at least half a dozen humans, humans that Sasha knew. He had to get them back.

He pushed his door open, following her into the cool night air. The road stretched empty before them, curving away into darkness. No sign of the box truck. No sign of anything but trees and the distant pinpricks of stars above. The scent of pine and damp earth filled his nostrils, familiar now after days in that forest.

Sasha had already popped the hood and was bent over the engine, her frustrated breaths coming out in small white puffs in the cool air. The moonlight caught her silhouette, painting her in silver and shadow. Her hair had fallen loose from its tie, cascading in wild waves around her shoulders. One hand was braced against the vehicle, her body leaning forward, curves outlined in the ghostly light.

She was beauty incarnate.

Fire sang in his blood, and he smelled a faint hint of smoke. He wanted her. Now. Tomorrow. Whenever she would have him.

But he'd already ruined that, hadn't he? Speaking of duty as if his most sacred duty wasn't standing right in front of him.

He moved closer, coming to stand beside her. Heat radiated from the engine, a complex maze of wires and metal parts that meant nothing to him. On Vemion, vehicles weren't nearly this complicated or finicky. He could handle the propulsion system on a battle cruiser, but this jumble of primitive technology might as well have been a puzzle box with no solution.

"Now would be a good time for you to pull out a sonic screwdriver to get us out of this mess," she said.

"A what?"

"Never mind." She reached in to touch something and then yanked her hand back with a curse, shaking it out and then putting her finger in her mouth. "Hot!"

Rook stepped closer, his body angling toward hers instinctively. He traced his hand up her arm, fingers barely skimming over her skin, and took her hand in his to examine it. "May I?" he asked. "I know heat."

She hesitated, her eyes searching his face in the dim light. For a moment, he thought she'd pull away, refuse his touch. But then she nodded, just once, and let her injured hand rest in his palm.

There was a red welt forming on her index finger, the skin already starting to blister. He brought her hand to his mouth, his gaze never leaving hers, and gently drew her finger between his lips. The taste of her skin exploded on his tongue, salt and something uniquely Sasha. He could feel her pulse fluttering wildly at her wrist, beating in time with his own racing heart.

Sasha gasped a little, her eyes widening, pupils dilating in the darkness.

Rook felt it go straight to his cock, hardening instantly at the small, broken sound she made. Heat flooded his body, his core temperature rising dangerously. The urge to pull her against him, to taste more than just her finger, to claim every inch of her skin was overwhelming.

He wanted more. Wanted it all.

Now.

Somewhere in the distance, he heard a reverberating boom. Sasha jerked her hand away from him, and he didn't try to fight her.

"We can't stay here." They both said it and then shared a smile.

Sasha looked around. All Rook saw were trees and plants. Above them was the night sky. But they might have been anywhere. The unfamiliar terrain all looked the same to him, dark shapes blending together in the shadows. He could feel the night cooling rapidly, the earlier warmth of the day giving way to a chill that would be uncomfortable for Sasha soon.

Sasha walked up the road a little bit, her boots crunching on loose gravel. She stared intently into the darkness, then turned and retraced her steps back to him, chewing her bottom lip in thought.

"What is it?" he asked.

"There aren't many places you could drive a box truck around here," she said. "Do you think they'd make their ..." she trailed off and shook her head before continuing, "my neighbors walk far on foot?"

"I'd bet my fire they wouldn't."

She nodded. "That's what I figured. Are you up for a midnight hike?"

Rook looked down at his mate, that fierce, stubborn woman who refused to let her friends be taken without a fight. Even when her mechanical beast had failed her, even when they were outgunned and outnumbered, she was still searching for a way forward. In that moment, he'd never been more certain of anything in his life.

"Lead the way," he said, already falling into step beside her, exactly where he belonged.

14

IT WAS crazy to follow a bunch of alien slaver dragons in her beat-up van.

It was even crazier to follow the assholes on foot.

Sasha tried to convince herself that this was all fine and that Rook would keep her safe if something went horribly wrong.

When something went horribly wrong.

"Damn it," he cursed and stumbled beside her.

Of course, only one of them seemed capable of moving easily through the woods. And it wasn't the dragon warrior.

The night air hung thick around them. Even with the threat of alien slavers lurking somewhere ahead, Sasha couldn't help but drink in the familiar beauty of her forest. The scent of evergreen and damp earth filled her lungs, and the gentle rustling of leaves overhead sounded like whispered secrets.

Even in the darkness, even with danger promising to find them, she felt a twisted comfort. That was her world, her territory. The woods had always been her refuge, the place she ran to when life got too heavy, too complicated, too human.

An owl hooted in the distance, its haunting call echoing through the trees. For a moment, she almost forgot they were tracking murderous aliens.

Almost.

The path narrowed, forcing them closer together as they picked their way over a fallen log. Rook's arm brushed against hers, warm even through the fabric of her sleeve. He steadied her with a light touch at her elbow when her boot slipped on a patch of moss.

If she squinted and ignored the mortal danger, it almost felt like a date. A nice nature hike with her boyfriend. The kind of thing normal people did. He'd point out constellations, she'd show him her favorite spot by the creek, and maybe they'd share a thermos of hot cocoa with just a hint of whiskey before making out on a pile of leaves. It was a pretty thought.

Except that Rook wasn't her boyfriend. He'd

made it annoyingly clear that nothing was going to happen between them.

She was a *distraction.*

And apparently, she was still distracting him. Because unless there was some sort of dragon social-norm she was misinterpreting, he kept eye-fucking her.

An eye-fuck was an eye-fuck, no matter the planet.

His gaze would linger when he thought she wasn't looking, tracing the curve of her jaw, the line of her neck, the shape of her body in the darkness. Heat would spark in those impossibly golden eyes before he'd force himself to look away, jaw clenched tight enough to crack teeth. Then, a minute later, his eyes would find her again, hungry and wanting and fighting it all at once.

For a guy who claimed to be focused on his mission, he sure spent a lot of time looking at her like she *was* the mission.

They continued in silence, the soft crunch of pine needles beneath their boots the only sound. Sasha tried to focus on the path ahead, on finding the slavers, on anything but the way her skin tingled whenever Rook came too close. She was failing miserably.

Suddenly, Rook grabbed Sasha's arm tightly.

She opened her mouth to ask what the hell he was doing when he placed his other hand over her lips.

Alright, she got the picture.

She nodded, but he still waited a beat before removing his hand.

Her finger tingled, the one that he'd basically sucked after she touched something she shouldn't have.

I know heat.

Yeah, right.

For someone who didn't want to be distracted, he wasn't acting like it.

Rook tugged her down into a crouch.

And now she was the distracted one.

His body was so close she could feel the unnatural warmth radiating from him, like standing next to a furnace on a winter day. His breathing was controlled but deep, his chest rising and falling in a hypnotic rhythm that made her too aware of her own rushed breaths. His hand still gripped her forearm, firm but not painful, the touch both protective and possessive.

They duckwalked forward. "There's a canyon

here," Sasha whispered. She got as close to him as she could, letting her lips brush his ear.

Rook stiffened.

His entire body went rigid, muscles coiling beneath his skin like a predator about to pounce. She felt a tremor run through him, a split-second shudder that spoke of restraint stretched to breaking. His head turned slightly toward her, their faces now inches apart. In the silvery moonlight, his eyes had a faint glow, pupils wide and dark against the gold. For one breathless moment, Sasha thought he might close that tiny gap between them.

Instead, he exhaled slowly, a wisp of actual smoke escaping between his clenched teeth.

"I thought you wanted high ground to defend," she kept talking.

It would be super embarrassing if all they were hiding from was a family of deer. Or even bears, really.

"If you're an army, yes," Rook agreed. "Though that doesn't matter much when we fight in our other forms. But a canyon is a great place to hide, especially with cloaking tech."

His other form. His *dragon* form.

The thought sent a shiver of fearful excitement down her spine. She tried to picture it: Rook, not as the imposing man beside her, but as something immense and scaled, with wings that could block out the moon and fire that could consume forests.

Would he still have those same golden eyes? Would he still look at her with that mixture of hunger and restraint?

She imagined what it might be like to touch scales instead of skin, to feel the heat of his dragon form beneath her palms. Would his wings unfurl like sails catching wind? What would it feel like to ride on his back, soaring above the treetops, the world spread out beneath them like a patchwork quilt?

It was terrifying and exhilarating, and she wanted it so much it made her chest ache.

"Can we see past this cloaking tech?" she asked, forcing her mind back to the task at hand.

"It's meant to disguise them from scans from my ship. They don't have the funds or generators big enough to visually cloak their camp."

"Oh. Okay. That's good." Probably.

They were up in the middle of nowhere. Sasha only hoped hikers had been staying away. Otherwise, they were making themselves treats for the slavers.

They crept forward, staying low, using the brush for cover. With each step, Rook positioned himself slightly in front of her, his broad shoulders effectively becoming a shield. When a branch snapped under her boot, he froze, arm extended across her chest to hold her back, his body coiled and ready to protect her.

It was sweet, in its way. Sweet and frustrating and a little condescending, like he thought she was made of glass. She'd survived plenty on her own before he came along with his fire and his muscles and his brooding alien nobility.

Still, something warm bloomed in her chest at his instinctual protectiveness. No one had ever treated her as something precious before, something worth shielding.

They reached the edge of the canyon, a wide gash in the earth that dropped away beneath them. Sasha squinted into the darkness, seeing nothing at first. Just more darkness, more trees, the faint glimmer of what might have been water at the bottom. But then she focused harder, letting her eyes adjust, and ... there.

Something was off about the shadows at the canyon floor. They weren't quite right, too structured, too solid against the fluid darkness of the forest. As her eyes adjusted, details emerged: the sleek, curved hull of what could only be a spaceship, gleaming faintly under the stars. Around it, artificial lights glowed, revealing a camp setup that looked bizarrely similar to the RV parks she knew so well. Parts of the ship itself seemed to have unfolded, extending outward like pop-outs on a luxury camper, creating additional living space.

"Are they camping outside? Why? They've got a whole ship."

"It's small."

It did not look small.

"And they want to see the sky." There was some wistfulness in his tone.

He'd been camping outside, too. Maybe it wasn't just about keeping his ship hidden.

There was something almost child-like in the way he said it, a glimpse of longing beneath the hard warrior exterior. She wondered what skies he was used to, what stars he called home. What did his planet look like at night? Did dragon lords sit around campfires and tell stories? Did they have s'mores on his planet?

The random thought nearly made her smile, despite everything.

They inched closer to the edge, seeking a better vantage point. Rook's hand found the small of her back, steadying her as they navigated the rocky outcropping. The contact sent warmth spreading across her skin, distractingly pleasant.

Suddenly, Sasha heard a mechanical whirr, and Rook tackled her to the ground.

The impact knocked the wind from her lungs, but she barely noticed the discomfort. Rook's body covered hers completely, his weight pressing her into the dirt and pine needles. One of his hands cradled the back of her head, protecting it even as he'd taken her down.

Rook rolled over and let out a stream of fire that hit the device dead on. It dropped to the ground with a dull thud.

It was about the size of a Roomba, if a Roomba could fly. Now it was just a melting husk of a ... something.

"What is that?"

"Surveillance drone," he said. He shot another wave of fire.

"Um ... are they going to notice that it's fried to a crisp?"

He looked down at the camp. "Unlikely. But that won't be the only one. If they're flying in a standard formation, we only have a few minutes before the next one comes our way. The humans are down there; they're being held by the ship. They wouldn't let them inside, it's too much of a risk one could get free and sabotage something."

"And you're about to charge in and rescue every-one?" she asked hopefully.

He gave her a soft smile. "We can't tonight."

"What if they take off before we—"

"There's a flight window. They can't leave for five more nights. Trust me, Sasha, we're going to get your friends back."

When he said it like that, she almost believed him.

15

VAN LIFE definitely looked cooler on a spaceship.

Sasha was probably supposed to be more awed, but she recognized the broad strokes of living in your vehicle. There was a small bed bolted to the wall on one side. A cockpit sat in front of a viewport that probably looked out at the stars under normal circumstances, but right then was just staring at blank screens.

Normal circumstances.

Ha!

A tiny kitchenette stood against one wall—if you could even call it that. A single burner, unrecogniz-able alien appliances with glowing buttons, and a basin that might have been a sink occupied the space. Everything was sleek and utilitarian, all curves and burnished metal with no sharp corners to bang into during turbulence. A narrow door was set into the far wall, probably a bathroom, though Sasha wondered if dragons needed bathrooms the same way humans did. Did they even poop?

She understood why he'd been camping outside. Even with the space to stretch out her arms, this craft was a bit ... dire.

"It's not much," Rook said, "but I don't need much."

He stood in the center of the ship, his massive frame making everything around him seem smaller. His eyes found hers across the space between them, hot and hungry, like he wanted to devour her whole. The air grew heavy, charged with something that made her skin prickle. Her lips felt suddenly dry, and she ran her tongue over them without thinking. His gaze tracked the movement, his jaw tightening.

"I thought you were a lord. Don't lords ..."

"Travel in luxury?" he guessed.

She shrugged.

"I am here to bring fugitives to justice. This isn't a pleasure cruise."

Pleasure.

She couldn't think about pleasure with him in

the room. If she thought about ... that word ... and him she might combust. Or do something he didn't want. He *said* he didn't want.

A man didn't look at a woman like Rook was looking at her if he didn't want to be kissed.

"How is your hand?" he asked.

She looked down at her palm. "What?"

"You injured it. Before."

And then he sucked on her like she was a lollipop. "It's fine."

Rook took a step towards her. "Let me see."

The space between them vanished too quickly. The ship had felt small before, but now it was tiny, claustrophobic in the best possible way. She was trapped with nowhere to run, cornered by a predator who watched her with gleaming eyes. Her heart beat fast in her chest, but her feet stayed planted.

She didn't want to escape. The thought of running never even crossed her mind.

Rook swiveled the cockpit chair around so it was facing the rest of the room. "Sit. Let me look." Going by his tone of voice, there was no telling him no.

She didn't want to tell him that anyway.

Sasha sank into the chair, the material cool against her thighs through her worn jeans. Rook dropped to one knee before her, a powerful being brought down to her level. There was something almost religious about it, something reverent. His proximity made her mouth dry. He was so close she could count his eyelashes, see the faint golden flecks in his irises that weren't quite human.

His fingers were gentle over her palm as he traced the lines. He held her like she was made of glass, turning her hand this way and that in the soft light of the ship. His touch moved up her wrist, the inside of her forearm, slowly exploring every inch of skin like he'd never felt anything so soft. His thumb stroked along her pulse point, and she knew he could feel her heartbeat racing. The burn on her finger was all but forgotten; she wasn't even sure he was looking at the right hand anymore. This had nothing to do with first aid and everything to do with touch, with contact, with need.

Sasha was tempted to say something cutting. *I wouldn't want to be a distraction.* It would stop this right in its tracks. It would serve Rook right.

She didn't say a word.

Rook's thumb traced circles on her wrist, and his eyes finally lifted to meet hers. The moment expanded, stretched, became everything. She could feel it in her bones—something cosmic, inevitable, a path laid out for them before either of them were born. His pupils dilated until the gold was nearly gone, and then he surged forward, his mouth claiming hers in a kiss that demanded everything.

If Sasha had any sarcastic rejoinders, they went out the door with any other conscious thought. Rook was kissing her. She might die.

Heat bloomed low in her belly, an aching need that radiated outward until she felt it in her fingertips. His lips were firm, insistent, a brand against her own. Her nerve endings lit up like sparklers, fizzling and sparking at every point of contact. Her back arched instinctively, seeking more of him, her body knowing what it wanted even as her brain short-circuited.

Rook tasted like smoke and spice, something alien and familiar all at once. His scent wrapped around her, woodsy and male with an undertone of heat like sun-warmed stone. She breathed him in, dizzy with it, drunk on the very essence of him.

Rook groaned against her mouth as she leaned into him. The sound vibrated through her bones. Her softness met his hardness. The fit was perfect, as if she'd been crafted to nestle against his chest. His hands found her waist, spanning it easily, his fingers nearly meeting at her back. He was strong enough to break her in two, and yet his touch remained gentle, reverent, controlled.

She needed closer to him. If she didn't feel his skin against hers, she might combust. And Rook was a dragon. He knew fire.

There was a fire in her, alright.

Sasha pushed off the chair, never breaking the kiss, and straddled his thighs. The new position brought her core flush against the hard ridge in his pants, and they both groaned at the contact. They tumbled to the floor in a tangle of limbs, Sasha clawing at his shirt, desperate to feel his skin against hers. Rook finally lost patience, grabbing the fabric and yanking it over his head in one fluid motion.

Holy hell. His chest was a masterpiece. Sculpted muscle rippled under golden skin, perfect ridges and valleys that begged to be traced with fingers, with tongue. A dusting of dark hair narrowed to a tantalizing trail that disappeared beneath his waistband. She reached out, hesitant, then laid her palm flat against his sternum. His heart thundered beneath her touch.

A sudden flash of self-consciousness hit her. She was just ... her. Human. Ordinary. But the hunger in Rook's eyes burned away any doubt. She reached for the hem of her shirt and pulled it off in one swift motion, tossing it aside.

Rook's groan was almost pained. "Beautiful," he breathed, the word barely audible.

His gaze was physical, a tangible caress that swept over her body and left goosebumps in its wake. No one had ever looked at her like that before, like she was precious and necessary, like he might die if he couldn't touch her. The sheer naked want in his eyes made her feel powerful and vulnerable all at once, seen in a way that stripped her bare even with half her clothes still on.

Rook surged up and flipped her over and suddenly, she was lying on her back on the chilly floor.

His mouth found hers again, hungry and demanding, before trailing down her neck in a series of biting kisses that made her gasp. Each spot his lips touched burned, a sweet sting that made her arch closer. His hands claimed her breasts, thumbs brushing over her nipples through the fabric of her bra. She whimpered, and he growled in response, the sound so inhuman it sent a shiver of excitement up her spine.

He pushed the fabric aside and lowered his head, taking one peak into his mouth. The wet heat of his tongue made her cry out, her hips lifting instinctively, seeking friction against him. He paid the same attention to the other breast, sucking and licking until she was writhing beneath him, her hands fisted in his hair, pulling him closer.

Rook pulled back a bit and grinned at her, and something in his expression shifted. The intensity was still there, but there was something else too—a playfulness, a lightness that made him suddenly seem less like an alien warrior and more like ... hers. Like he belonged to her, at least for now. The realization stole her breath.

His hands moved to the waistband of her jeans, popping the button and dragging the zipper down with agonizing slowness. Sasha lifted her hips, helping him strip them away, too far gone for embarrassment. She needed him with a desperation that bordered on pain, an emptiness that demanded to be filled.

The cool air of the ship kissed her newly bared skin, making her shiver—or maybe that was the weight of Rook's gaze as he drank in the sight of her in nothing but her underwear. Every inch of her felt alive, hypersensitive. The metal floor pressed cold against her back, a sharp contrast to the heat of Rook's body hovering over her. His scent surrounded her, filled her lungs with each panting breath. Her thoughts fractured, scattered, reduced to primal need —touch, take, closer, more.

Rook settled in between her thighs, his broad shoulders pushing them wider. His breath ghosted over her most sensitive spot, hot and promising through the thin fabric still covering her. Then his tongue pressed against her.

Sasha let out a loud moan, the sound bouncing off the metal walls of the ship. There was no holding back, no hiding what he did to her.

He hooked his fingers in the waistband and drew her underwear down and off, his eyes never leaving the newly revealed flesh. Then his mouth was on her, his tongue parting her folds in one long, devastating lick. Pleasure shot through her, sharp and bright, making her gasp. He hummed against her, the vibration adding another layer of sensation that made her thighs tremble.

Sasha lost herself in the feel of him, in the wet heat of his mouth working her with single-minded determination. Her fingers tangled in his hair, holding him to her, guiding him where she needed him most. Her hips lifted into each stroke of his tongue, shameless in her pursuit of pleasure. The pressure built at the base of her spine, a coiling tension that wound tighter with each pass of his talented mouth.

He didn't let up, didn't give her a moment to catch her breath. His hands gripped her thighs, keeping her spread for his feast. When he closed his lips around her swollen bud and sucked, the tension snapped. She came with a cry, her body bowing off the floor, pleasure crashing through her in waves that left her gasping for air.

She must have been sex-high because Sasha could have sworn that there were little flames in Rook's eyes and smoke coming off his skin. His chin was wet with the evidence of her arousal.

Rook climbed up Sasha's body, his movements slow and predatory. He slipped a finger inside her, groaning at how wet she was, how easily she accepted him. A second finger joined the first, stretching her, preparing her for him. His thumb circled her sensitive nub, drawing out the aftershocks of her orgasm and building her toward another.

"I need you," he groaned it like a prayer.

"Yes."

Slowly and with great care, Rook entered her, stretching her in the most delicious way. It was primal, it was physical, it was perfect. The slide of him inside her made them both gasp. He fit as if he'd been made for her, filling every empty space, sating a hunger she hadn't known she had.

Sasha's hands roamed over his back, feeling the play of muscles under her palms as he began to move. Each thrust sent sparks of pleasure racing through her veins. The sound of their breathing, ragged and desperate, filled the small space. The scent of them together, sweat and sex and something almost like smoke, made her dizzy. The taste of him lingered on her lips, spice and heat. Every sense was overwhelmed, consumed by him, by them, by this moment that felt both impossible and inevitable.

Her body responded to his as if they'd done this a thousand times before, finding a rhythm that built and built until she was clinging to him, her nails digging into his shoulders. Rook's movements grew more urgent, more desperate, his control finally slipping. His forehead pressed against hers, his eyes locked with hers, golden and burning with something that looked like worship.

She felt the tension building again, that sweet pressure at the base of her spine. Rook's hand slipped between them, his thumb finding that perfect spot, and she shattered again, crying out his name. Her body clenched around him, pulling him deeper, and he followed her over the edge with a roar that was more dragon than man, his hips stuttering against hers as he found his release.

It was perfect. So perfect Sasha was pretty sure she was dreaming. Then Rook said the words no girl wants to hear while her body was still rippling with pleasure.

"There's something I have to tell you."

16

FROM THE WARY look on his mate's face, Rook suspected he had said something wrong.

A languid satisfaction still thrummed through his body, his muscles loose and heavy with pleasure. His skin felt hypersensitive, every nerve ending alive in the aftermath of their joining. The taste of her lingered on his tongue, sweet and addictive.

Her scent surrounded him, a heady mix of arousal and something uniquely Sasha that made his dragon purr with contentment. He wanted to pull her back against his chest, to feel her heartbeat against his ribs, to bury his face in her hair and breathe her in until she was part of him. The urge to mark her, to claim her completely, pulsed beneath his skin like a second heart-beat. Mine, his dragon whispered. Finally, utterly mine.

But going any further without telling her the truth felt like a lie. He shouldn't have taken her like this without saying. She deserved to know.

He had crossed the galaxy and found her. He refused to lose her from simply misspeaking.

Oh, the Royal Matchmaker would be laughing at him now. He'd stormed out of her office, determined to never let fate interfere.

And now ...

Sasha scooped his shirt off the floor and pulled it on, crossing her arms under her breasts.

Satisfaction rippled through him at the sight of her in his clothes. The black fabric swallowed her small frame, the sleeves hanging past her fingertips, the hem hitting mid-thigh. She looked claimed, marked as his in the most primitive way possible. His scent would cling to her skin now, a subtle announcement to any other male who came near that she was taken. Protected. His. The possessive heat that flared in his chest was so intense it took his breath away.

"If you're going to tell me this was a mistake, just say something already," Sasha snapped.

"What? No! I wouldn't—" But he had. Days ago, after that kiss. The things he'd said then were dishonorable. He'd rejected Sasha because he could feel the undeniable pull between them.

He wasn't denying it any longer.

"Either talk or put pants on, Rook."

Right.

He sat on the edge of the bed and tried not to feel disappointed when Sasha moved farther towards the wall to put space between them. She was fully sitting up now and looking at him like he might eat her.

Not like *that*.

"I told you that my fire could not harm you." It was best to start with the basics.

"Yes ..." Sasha had drawn her knees up to her chest, making herself as small as possible in the narrow space. Her shoulders were rigid, every muscle coiled like she was ready to bolt. But there was nowhere to go. His bulk blocked the only exit from the sleeping alcove, and she'd have to climb over him to escape. Her eyes darted from his face to the door and back again, calculating. The wariness in her green gaze made his chest ache.

"I didn't tell you why."

"I noticed that," she grumbled.

He wanted to kiss her right then. He had a feeling she might bite him if he tried.

"I need you to trust me. Put your hands out."

"Rook ..."

"Please." He would lay down his life for her, his very soul. But he needed her to do this, to understand.

Sasha hesitated, her fingers curling into fists against her shins. She studied his face for a long moment, searching for something that would tell her whether to trust him or run. Whatever she saw there must have convinced her, because she slowly uncurled and extended her hands toward him, palms up. Her fingers trembled slightly, but whether from fear or the lingering effects of their lovemaking, he couldn't tell.

Rook summoned his fire, and Sasha gasped. He held his hand out over hers, the fire hovering just an inch from her skin. The flames danced between his fingers, casting golden light across her face. "Do you feel that?" he asked.

"It tickles. But it's not hot. Why?"

He tipped his hand over and released the fire. As close as it was to her skin, it answered the call within her instead of retreating back into him.

Sasha nearly ripped her hands back in shock.

"Careful!" said Rook. "You're immune to my fire. The bed isn't."

"Jesus! Warn a girl." She cupped the fire like it was a baby animal, her movements instinctive and sure despite her startled words. The flames curled around her fingers like living silk, responding to her touch with an eagerness that made Rook's breath catch. "What is this? Why? How?"

"My fire is yours," he said. There were no formal vows, but it felt that way when he said it. The words carried weight, a solemn promise that settled deep in his bones. "When you hold it, you control it. You can summon it from my soul and wield it as your own. When I'm in my other form, you can speak to my mind. There is only one person in the universe that this is true for."

Sasha carefully pulled her hands apart and let the fire flow between them in a graceful ribbon of light. She was a natural, her movements confident as she shaped the flames into spirals and loops. The fire obeyed her every whim, eager to please its new mistress. "Why, Rook?"

"You are my mate."

The words hung in the air between them, heavy with implication. Sasha went very still, the fire frozen in her palms as if even the flames were holding their breath. Her eyes widened, pupils dilating with shock. For a heartbeat, she looked like she'd forgotten how to breathe.

She clapped her hands together, and the fire disappeared. "What? How?"

"It's fate," was his only explanation.

"We're from different *planets*."

"Fate doesn't care."

Sasha pushed at his shoulder with both hands, her touch burning through him even as she tried to create distance.

"Okay, you really need to put pants on now." She scrambled around him and swung her legs off the bed, looking for her own pants, which she found hanging off the armrest of the chair. She pulled them on with jerky, agitated movements, her face flushed with something that might have been panic. Once dressed, she started pacing the narrow confines of the ship like a caged animal. "I can't be your mate. I'm just ... I'm— I'm just some trail guide who lives in her van. You're a fucking dragon! And a lord! And an alien." She clutched her head, fingers tangling in her disheveled hair.

Rook didn't put on his pants. Instead, he crossed the room in two strides and wrapped his arms around her, pulling her back against his chest. She fit perfectly against him, her body molding to his as if they'd been made for each other. Which, he supposed, they had. "You are wonderful. And brave. And beautiful. You know the world around you better than anyone I've ever met. I am proud to call you my mate. If you'll have—"

It would have been a beautiful declaration.

If the monitoring sensor he'd left outside of the slaver's camp hadn't chosen that moment to shrill through the ship and shatter their peace.

17

MATE.

Rook was her mate.

She was Rook's mate.

Mates were a thing.

What the fuck?

Sasha really needed to be thinking about the mission ahead of her and not the life-altering revelations that Rook had made two hours ago. That was what a proper warrior would do.

But she was no warrior. She was just an adventure guide who had been sucked into a world she'd never imagined could exist.

And now she was ...

Fuck!

Sasha's fingers dug into the brittle rock as she

scaled the side of the canyon. Each handhold felt uncertain, crumbling slightly beneath her grip. Sweat trickled down her back despite the cool night air, her shirt sticking uncomfortably to her skin. A rock skittered loose beneath her boot, tumbling down into darkness.

She froze, holding her breath.

No shouts of alarm came from below. No sudden flare of alien fire lit up the night. Just the soft whisper of wind through the pines and the distant call of a night bird.

Her muscles trembled with the effort of holding herself still. She was used to hiking, to guiding tourists through challenging terrain, but rock climbing had never been her specialty. And she'd certainly never done it while sneaking into an alien dragon slaver camp.

Alone.

Sasha should have been glad to be alone. That had always been her preference, hadn't it? Self-reliance was her religion. But right now, she could really use Rook's steady presence, his warmth at her back, his ridiculous confidence that made impossible things seem manageable.

Instead, she had his absence and the echo of his words.

You're my mate.

She pushed the thought away and resumed climbing, one painful inch at a time.

It was obvious he hadn't wanted her to come. Some facial expressions were universal.

After the alarm had gone off, they'd jumped into action. Rook had stared at her as she pulled on her boots and pulled her gun out of her backpack.

"Why do you have that?" he asked.

"We saw the nice kind of bears the other day. Grizzlies, on the other hand ..." She wasn't sure a Glock would be enough to damage a grizzly bear, but it was better than nothing.

And against an alien dragon?

Sasha had no idea. They were shaped like humans. She'd seen Rook get hurt like a human. Bullets probably impacted them like they would a human.

She just didn't know if she could shoot someone person-shaped, no matter how heinous their crimes.

The gun was holstered at her side. And now she had another weapon. Rook's fire. Theoretically. She had no idea how to summon it or use it, and Rook didn't have time to teach her.

The alarm he'd set indicated that some number of the slavers had left camp. Maybe they were going to find more victims, maybe they needed supplies, maybe they were just stretching their legs. Whatever the reason, it meant that there were fewer slavers in the camp guarding Sasha's neighbors.

Now was the perfect time to strike.

The plan was as simple as could be. Rook would cause a distraction at the north end of the camp and summon as many of the slavers to him as he could. Then, when she saw his signal, Sasha would sneak in and find the humans.

She was doing her best to ignore the memory of Erik going up in flames. Sasha was immune to Rook's fire, not anyone else's.

Sasha finally reached the top of the canyon ridge, her hands raw and scraped from the climb. She flattened herself against the rocky ground, crawling forward on her belly until she could peer down into the depression below.

The slaver camp sprawled beneath her like a nightmarish carnival. Portable lights cast eerie blue-white circles on the packed dirt, illuminating the sleek curves of their ship and the cluster of tents around it. Shadows moved between structures, tall figures with unnaturally fluid grace. She counted one, two, three ... eight of them total. Was that fewer than before? She couldn't tell. The shapes kept moving, merging with shadows, then reappearing elsewhere.

Her heart pounded hard. Eight dragon slavers against one human woman. The math wasn't promising.

A sound caught her attention, something between a sob and a whimper. Her eyes found its source: a large tent set apart from the others, guarded by two towering figures in those shiny black uniforms. They stood like sentinels, their posture rigid, hands clasped behind their backs. Even from that distance, she could see the golden gleam of their eyes, scanning the perimeter.

That had to be where they were keeping the captives. Her neighbors. People who'd waved to her in the campground, shared beers around communal fire pits, complained about the shower temperature.

Sasha's hand drifted to her Glock, fingers brushing the grip. The metal was cool against her palm, reassuring in its solid presence. She took a deep breath.

I can handle two, she told herself firmly. *I've faced worse.*

Though she wasn't sure that was true anymore. Bears didn't throw fireballs.

Then, fire.

A roaring wall of flame erupted at the northern edge of the camp, leaping thirty feet into the air. The heat from it washed over her face even at that distance, and she instinctively ducked lower against the ground. An alarm blared through the camp, a high-pitched wailing that set her teeth on edge.

For a terrifying moment, nothing happened. Then two slavers broke away from their positions, running toward the conflagration with fluid, predatory grace. A third followed, moving more cautiously.

The rest remained at their posts, including the guards at the prisoner tent.

Come on, Sasha silently urged. *Take the bait.*

Anxiety coiled in her stomach. What if Rook's plan wouldn't work? What if she was stuck up there, watching uselessly while he fought alone?

A massive explosion ripped through the air, so violent it shook the ground beneath her. She clapped her hands over her ears, wincing as a shower of debris and sparks rained down on the camp. The remaining slavers shouted to each other in their strange, guttural language, voices sharp with alarm.

One by one, they abandoned their posts, racing toward the growing chaos at the north end. Even the guards at the prisoner tent seemed torn, their heads swiveling between their duty and the battle unfolding in the distance.

Sasha watched with her breath held, muscles tensed and ready to move. She was still waiting for Rook's signal. Her body vibrated with the need to rush in, to help, to do something, but she knew rushing without coordination would only make things worse.

The slavers in front of the human's tent were arguing. Sasha watched as one turned and ran towards the chaos.

One down. One left.

She could handle one.

Then three booms, one right after the other.

Her sign.

Sasha was moving before her brain fully registered the signal. She slid down the loose dirt of the canyon wall, half-climbing, half-falling, her hands grabbing at sparse vegetation to slow her descent. Rocks tumbled beside her, a miniature avalanche that she prayed wouldn't attract attention.

Her boots hit the canyon floor with a jarring impact that shot pain up her shins. No time to recover. She darted from shadow to shadow, crouching behind stacks of metal crates and the curved walls of alien tents. The smell of smoke and something chemical hung thick in the air, coating the back of her throat.

Every few seconds, she froze, listening for footsteps or alien voices. The sounds of battle grew louder from the north end, punctuated by what could only be Rook's roars of challenge.

She pulled out her gun with shaking hands.

Steady. You need to be steady.

She crept forward, keeping low, her eyes darting from shadow to shadow. More explosions rocked the camp, and she saw slavers running toward the source, their forms silhouetted against the fiery glow. More than she'd expected. It seemed like they were all converging on the northern perimeter.

With a jolt, she realized why: they all wanted the glory of taking down a dragon lord. Rook wasn't just a threat, he was a prize.

She wasn't going to let that happen.

Sasha rounded the corner of a tent, her mind fixed on the prisoners just yards away, when a solid wall of muscle slammed into her. She stumbled backward, raising her gun on pure instinct as she found herself face-to-face with one of the slavers.

His eyes widened, glowing yellow with shock that matched her own. For a heartbeat, they stared at each other, frozen in mutual surprise. Then his hand rose, fingers splaying as a weak, sputtering flame flickered to life in his palm.

Sasha didn't think. Her finger squeezed the trigger.

The gun kicked in her hand, the report deafening in the close quarters. The slaver's head snapped back, a look of stunned disbelief crossing his features before he crumpled to the ground.

He went down hard.

Bile rose in Sasha's throat, the sudden need to barf. Oh, god. She *shot* him.

Her hands trembled violently now, the gun suddenly too heavy. She'd never shot anything but paper targets. Never seen that moment when a bullet found flesh, when life drained from eyes.

But she couldn't stop. Not now. Not when she was so close.

She staggered a few feet away, dropped to her knees, and vomited onto the packed dirt. Her stomach heaved, emptying itself in painful spasms. When there was nothing left, she wiped her mouth with the back of her hand, the sour taste lingering on her tongue.

Get up. Keep going. They need you.

Somehow, she made it to the prisoner tent, now

abandoned by its guards. The canvas flap hung partially open, revealing darkness within.

She opened the flap and was immediately assaulted by a muddy shoe.

"Stay the fuck away from us!" Janice screamed.

Sasha raised her hands, which may have looked a bit threatening since she was still holding her gun. "I'm here to rescue you."

Janice gave her an appraising look. "Took you long enough."

Janice was there. And Vanessa, along with a few of the others she'd seen on MISSING posters. There were also five others who'd been taken yesterday. Sasha didn't know all of their names, but she recognized most of the faces.

"Come on," she said. "We need to hurry."

She holstered her gun and pulled a small pocketknife from her boot, sawing through the crude restraints binding their wrists and ankles. Some of the captives were drugged, their movements sluggish, eyes unfocused. Others helped Sasha, working in frantic silence to free everyone. Vanessa, her nurse's training kicking in, checked each person for injuries as they were released.

"Can you walk?" Sasha asked a teenage boy whose ankle was swollen to twice its normal size.

"I'll fucking crawl if I have to," he spat, struggling to his feet.

They moved as a ragged group out of the tent, Sasha in the lead, Janice bringing up the rear. The camp was eerily deserted, most of the slavers drawn to the battle on the north side. The sounds from that direction had changed, though. Fewer explosions now, more shouts and an occasional roar that made the hair on Sasha's arms stand up.

Was Rook winning? Losing? The decrease in chaos made her stomach knot with worry.

"This way," she hissed, pointing toward the tree line. "Stay low and quiet."

They were almost home free. If they made it to the tree line, Sasha was sure they could disappear, and the dragons wouldn't ever find them.

The group moved as quickly as they could, half-running, half-stumbling across the open ground. Twenty yards to go. Fifteen. Ten.

Behind her, Sasha heard a thud and a cry of pain. She whirled to see Janice sprawled on the ground, clutching her ankle, face twisted in agony.

"Keep going!" Sasha shouted to the others, who hesitated only briefly before continuing their desperate dash for the trees.

Sasha ran back to Janice, dropping to her knees beside the older woman.

"You're okay," she said, helping Janice to her feet. "We're almost there."

Then a line of fire appeared right in front of her, the heat hot enough to singe her hands.

"I don't think you're going anywhere."

18

FIRE RAGED AROUND ROOK, the natural playground of any dragon. The battle was chaos and fury.

The first slaver came at him with a whip of flame that crackled through the air like lightning. Rook deflected it with a wall of his own fire, the heat sliding off his skin harmlessly, and twisted his wrist to send the heat snapping back. It caught the slaver across the chest, and he went down with a scream that cut through the night.

These weren't warriors. They fought like street brawlers, all raw power and no finesse. Their flames were wild, uncontrolled, wasted on flashy displays instead of precision strikes.

At the Royal Academy, instructors would have beaten such sloppy technique out of them in the first week. But what they lacked in skill, they made up for in numbers and desperation.

A jet of blue-white fire erupted from his left. Rook threw his shoulder back and out of the way as the flame gusted past him, close enough to singe the air where his head had been. He spun, his own fire already forming in his palm, and hurled it at the attacker. The slaver barely managed to throw up a shield of his own flames in time.

Rook was the more skilled fighter, but it was one on ten, and the slavers just needed to get lucky.

Two more slavers circled around behind him, trying to flank him while he was engaged with the others. Rook could hear their boots scraping against the rocky ground, could smell the acrid tang of their fire building. He feinted left, then dove right, rolling across the dirt as twin streams of flame crossed where he'd been standing.

The heat was tremendous. Even for a dragon, the combined output of so many fires was like standing in a furnace. Sweat beaded on his forehead, ran down his spine. His shirt stuck to his back, the fabric already singed in places. The air itself seemed to shimmer with the intensity.

Stalling was the only thing keeping Sasha safe.

He'd managed to draw ten of them to his side of

the camp. Those were better odds for Sasha, but it meant he was badly outnumbered there. Every second that passed increased the chances that one of their wild attacks would find its mark.

A spear of concentrated flame shot past his ear, so close he could smell his own hair burning. Another slaver had climbed onto a stack of supply crates, giving him the high ground. Rook cursed and sent a wave of fire rushing up the makeshift platform. The crates caught instantly, metal groaning as it warped in the heat. The slaver leaped clear just as the whole structure collapsed in a shower of sparks.

The acrid smoke was getting thicker, making his eyes water. It carried the smell of melting plastic and scorched metal, harsh chemical stenches that had no place in those woods. Soon, the whole camp would be visible from miles away, a beacon that would draw unwanted human attention.

If only he could shift into his other form, the battle would be over in seconds. But once he shifted, some of the slavers were sure to follow. And that would lead to disaster.

A dragon battle in the skies above Earth would be impossible to hide or explain away. The humans had primitive aircraft, but they also had cameras, satellites, social media. Within hours, footage would be spreading across their global networks. The existence of dragons would be exposed, and King Venin would want an explanation for Rook's sloppiness.

He really didn't want to answer to his uncle.

So he fought in his human form, limited and vulnerable, while his dragon raged beneath his skin like a caged beast.

Two more slavers coordinated their attack, coming at him from opposite sides with walls of flame that would meet in the middle. Rook dropped to the ground and rolled, feeling the heat pass over him like the breath of a furnace. He came up with fire already building in both hands and let it loose in a wide arc that forced both attackers to leap backward.

One of them wasn't fast enough. Rook's flames caught him across the legs, and he went down hard, rolling in the dirt to try to extinguish the fire eating at his uniform. The smell of burning flesh joined the chemical reek in the air.

A blade of pure fire whistled past Rook's head, so close it left his skin tingling. Another slaver had shaped his flames into a cutting weapon, something that took real skill. This one had at least some training, unlike the others. Rook studied his stance, the way he held his hands, and recognized techniques from the outer colonies. Military, probably, or at least paramilitary.

That one would be dangerous.

The slaver attacked again, his fire-blade extending and contracting like a living thing. Rook dodged back, then forward, staying just out of range while he looked for an opening. The blade carved through the air where he'd been, leaving trails of sparks that faded slowly.

Then the slaver overextended, putting too much power into a downward strike that left him momentarily off-balance. Rook stepped inside his guard and drove his fist into the man's solar plexus, channeling fire through the punch. The slaver doubled over, gasping, and Rook's follow-up blast sent him flying backward into a tree.

Seven down. Three still moving, but they were hanging back now, more cautious. They'd seen what happened to their companions who got too close. The smart play would be to retreat, regroup, come back with better tactics.

But slavers weren't known for their intelligence.

Sasha screamed.

The sound cut through the roar of flames and the crack of burning wood like a knife through his heart. It was pure terror, raw and desperate, and it made every protective instinct he possessed flare to life. His dragon clawed at his consciousness, demanding to be released, demanding blood.

Only years of training kept Rook from freezing at the sound of his mate's terror. He blasted the closest slaver with more fire, not bothering to aim carefully, just wanting him down and out of the way. The man stumbled backward, flames licking at his armor, and Rook took off running.

If Sasha was in trouble, there was no use keeping up the distraction.

He sprinted through the camp, weaving between tents and supply caches, his boots pounding against the packed earth. The sounds of battle faded behind him as the remaining slavers tried to decide whether to follow or regroup. Let them wonder. All that mattered was reaching Sasha.

The camp was nearly deserted. His plan had worked almost too well. Scattered equipment lay abandoned where the slavers had dropped it in their rush to join the fight. A pot of something that might have been food still bubbled over a small heating element, filling the air with an alien spice that reminded him of home.

But near the center of camp where the humans were being held captive, one of the slavers he recognized from earlier stood waiting. The one with the scar that ran from his jaw to his temple, the leader who'd been coordinating their movements. He had his arm around Sasha's throat, holding her against his chest like a shield.

The slaver had a ball of fire in his other hand. Not touching Sasha, but close enough to make the threat obvious. Close enough that one wrong move would end everything.

"Lord Rook," said the slaver. "So kind of you to join us."

Rook's eyes found Sasha's face, saw the fear there but also the anger. Her jaw was set in that stubborn line he was coming to know so well. She wasn't broken, wasn't giving up, even with death hovering inches from her skin.

He didn't see the other humans anywhere. The tent that had held them stood empty, its flap hanging open. He didn't know if that meant she'd gotten them out safely or if they were hidden elsewhere, still captive. The uncertainty gnawed at him, but he couldn't let it show. Any sign of weakness would only make things worse.

Rook raised a hand in a gesture of peace, forcing his voice to remain calm and level. "There's no need to harm the human. Let her go."

One wrong word and she would go up in flames. He could hear the other slavers approaching from behind, their footsteps crunching on gravel and debris, but they stayed in a loose circle out of the range of the scarred man's flame. Smart. They knew who was in charge here.

It was clear who the leader was.

"Are you so desperate that you're teaming up with cattle?" the slaver asked, his tone mocking, superior. The fire in his hand pulsed brighter, casting dancing shadows across his scarred face. "If you were so eager for a win, I might have thrown a few of these useless idiots your way as a favor."

"Hey!" he heard one of the useless idiots shout from somewhere behind the slavers before someone shushed him.

Rook kept his expression neutral, even as rage built in his chest like molten lava. Cattle. As if Sasha were nothing more than livestock, something to be bought and sold and disposed of when no longer useful. The slaver had no idea what he was holding, no concept of the bond that tied her to Rook's very soul.

"It's over," Rook told him, putting as much authority into his voice as he could muster. As a dragon lord, it was a lot.

The command rang through the air like a bell, carrying years of breeding and training, the weight of royal blood and absolute power. He'd used that voice to quell riots, to cow enemy generals, to make lesser dragons prostrate themselves in submission. It was the voice of someone who expected to be obeyed without question.

He could sense a mood shift around him, a wavering in the slavers' confidence. They were criminals and outcasts, but they were still Vemion dragons. The instinctive response to authority was bred into their bones just as surely as their fire. Several of them shifted uncomfortably, their flames flickering lower.

It was clear the scarred slaver had the upper hand with his hostage, but Rook was very convincing. The other slavers began to glance between their leader and the dragon lord, uncertainty creeping into their postures.

The scarred slaver felt it too, that erosion of his control. His grip on Sasha tightened, and he moved his fire closer to her face. She tried to jerk her head back, but he had much too tight a hold on her. The flames reflected in her eyes, turning them molten gold.

The slaver threw his head back and laughed, the

sound harsh and grating in the smoky air. "Oh, you think you still have power here? You think your bloodline means anything when I'm the one holding the cards?"

"If one of you is going to light me on fire, I'd rather him burn us both!" Sasha spat at the slaver, her voice rough but defiant.

His mate was a vicious thing.

His mate.

The word echoed in his mind with sudden, perfect clarity. She wasn't just some human he was trying to protect. She was his fated partner, the other half of his soul, the one person in all the universe who could touch his fire and remain unharmed.

Oh.

Understanding flooded through him like sunrise after the longest night.

Rook summoned his flame and blasted it straight at the slaver and Sasha.

The fire erupted from his hands in a river of molten heat that engulfed both figures. The scarred slaver's eyes went wide with shock, then pain, as the flames found every gap in his armor and poured through. His own fire sputtered and died as he lost concentration, his scream echoing across the camp.

But Sasha stood untouched in the heart of the

inferno. The flames parted around her like water around a stone, caressing her skin without leaving so much as a mark. Her hair whipped in the supernatural wind of the fire, but she remained unharmed, protected by forces older than civilization.

The slaver's grip loosened as the flames consumed him, and Sasha pulled free, stumbling away from his collapsing form. He hit the ground hard, his body already beginning to crumble to ash.

Before the rest of the slavers could figure out what was going on, Rook turned on them and let his flame loose.

Confusion rippled through their ranks like a physical thing. They'd just seen their leader burn while his hostage walked away unscathed. It violated everything they thought they knew about fire, about dragons, about the natural order. Some of them took half-hearted steps backward, others raised their hands to summon their own flames, but none of them moved fast enough.

Rook's fire swept through them like a scythe through wheat. It was chaos for a moment, but only just. The gathered slavers weren't expecting the attack and didn't have time to defend against it. They'd been focused on their leader's confrontation, watching the drama unfold, when death came calling in a wave of superheated air.

One by one, they fell. Some tried to run, others attempted to fight back with desperate bursts of flame, but Rook's fire was too strong, too precise. He'd been trained by the best masters in the galaxy, had studied the art of combat since he could walk. These street thugs and pirates were no match for a dragon lord in full fury.

In just a minute or two, they were all dead.

The camp fell silent except for the crackle of dying flames and the distant hoot of an owl. Smoke drifted between the tents like fog, carrying the acrid smell of melted metal and worse things. Rook stood in the center of it all, his chest heaving, fire still dancing along his fingertips.

Rook turned his back on the slavers' ashes, but Sasha was gone.

Fear struck true for a moment, sharp and cold in his chest. Had he somehow burnt his mate after all? Had the scarred slaver gotten in one lucky shot before the end? The possibility made his blood turn to ice, his dragon roaring in anguish at the thought of losing her.

Then he heard shrill human voices coming from the edge of the camp and followed the sound to where Sasha was speaking with an older woman in the same patient, calming tone one would use with a panicked animal.

"He's a monster!" the older woman yelled, pointing a shaking finger in Rook's direction. "Did you see what he did? Fire! From his hands! That's not natural!"

"He's my boyfriend, Janice, it's cool," his mate was saying, her voice steady and reassuring even as she shot Rook a look that was part exasperation, part something that might have been fondness.

Boyfriend? Humans had such strange ways of saying things. The term seemed inadequate to describe what they were to each other, but he supposed it was better than trying to explain the concept of fated mates to a group of traumatized humans.

Sasha gave him a look that was almost bashful, one shoulder lifting in a small shrug. "This is your mess to clean up, honey bear."

Honey bear? That was even stranger than boyfriend. He made a mental note to ask her about human endearments later, when they weren't surrounded by witnesses and the smoking ruins of a slaver camp.

But cleaning up was simpler than the fight. Rook

had plenty of Earth money stashed on his ship, just in case he needed bribes or cash on hand for his mission. The humans who had been captured were happy to agree to silence in exchange for his reserves, especially when they saw the thick stacks of bills.

Money, it seemed, was a universal language.

"Did you really give each of them fifty grand in small bills?" Sasha demanded after they'd repurposed the box truck to pick up the money and then drop the humans back near their home with a story about gas leaks and hallucinations that might hold up to casual scrutiny.

"Is that not enough?" The conversions between Vemion gold and Earth dollars wasn't exact, and he'd never been good with the local currency anyway. "It's all I had."

Sasha snorted, a sound that was half laughter, half disbelief. "It's more than any of them make in a year."

He'd have to remember that for future reference. Apparently, his casual spending money was a fortune by human standards. No wonder they'd agreed to keep quiet so readily.

But there was still work to do. The slaver camp needed to be completely destroyed, every trace of alien technology melted down or vaporized. Their ship would have to be buried or teleported into deep space. Any evidence that might lead investigators to ask uncomfortable questions had to be eliminated.

It took hours, but finally, the canyon looked like nothing more than a natural clearing. The ship was gone, transported to the heart of a star. The tents and equipment had been reduced to unrecognizable slag. Even the scorch marks from the battle had been carefully obscured.

When it was finished, they sat alone in the box truck in a roadside parking area, watching the sun rise through the windshield. Sasha leaned against him, her head on his shoulder, and Rook put an arm around her, breathing in the scent of her hair. She smelled like smoke and pine needles and something uniquely her that made his dragon purr with contentment.

"You gave away all your cash," she said quietly. "So you're leaving?"

The question hung in the air between them, heavy with unspoken implications. She wasn't asking about his mission or his duties as a dragon lord. She was asking about them, about what came next, about whether this was goodbye.

"My job on Earth is done."

He'd come to that planet as a hunter, tracking

fugitives who'd escaped Vemion justice. He'd expected to capture or kill them and return home with another successful mission added to his record. He'd never imagined he'd find something far more valuable than justice or duty.

He'd found the other half of his soul, the woman who could walk through his fire and emerge unscathed, the mate he'd never dared to hope for.

But what did that mean for her? She had a life here, a job, friends, a whole world that was familiar and safe. What right did he have to ask her to leave it all behind?

He was her mate.

He had every right.

"Come home with me. To Vemion."

OF COURSE SHE SAID YES.

One year later, and Sasha didn't regret it. The ride from Earth to Vemion had been a bit cramped. But being stuck on a small ship with just a tiny bed had led to some ... creative uses of space.

And once they landed, *cramped* was the last thing they were.

Her boyfriend lived in a freaking palace.

He insisted it was a minor country estate, but to someone who'd been dreaming of studio apartments when he came into her life, the place might as well have been Versailles.

Not that Sasha was complaining.

He had grounds around his not-palace that were almost as good as the wilderness back home. The trees weren't quite right—the bark was too smooth, the leaves a shade of green that didn't exist on Earth —but they still whispered secrets when the wind moved through them. The undergrowth was dense enough to lose herself in, thick with ferns that brushed her knees and flowering vines that perfumed the air with something like jasmine crossed with cinnamon.

She'd found a stream that morning, narrow but swift, cutting through moss-covered rocks in a way that reminded her of the woods where they'd first kissed. The water was clearer than anything she'd seen on Earth, so transparent she could count the pebbles on the bottom from twenty feet away. She'd knelt beside it and splashed some on her face, tasting the mineral sweetness on her lips.

The path wound deeper into the woods, her boots silent on the cushion of fallen leaves. Overhead, the canopy filtered the sunlight into dappled patterns that shifted and danced with each breath of wind. Birds called from the branches—not quite the same songs she knew from home, but close enough to make her chest ache with nostalgia.

Vemion was a lot like Earth, strangely enough. Rook had mentioned something about convergent evolution and similar atmospheric conditions, but Sasha suspected it was simpler than that. Maybe the universe just had a soft spot for green places where people could get lost and find themselves again.

She paused beside a tree whose trunk was wider than her van had been, pressing her palm against the bark. It was warm beneath her touch, almost like it had a pulse. The sensation traveled up her arm, a gentle hum that made her think of Rook's fire, controlled and comforting.

A shadow passed overhead, too large and too purposeful to be a cloud.

Sasha tipped her head up and saw a dragon flying. Massive wings beat against the pale blue sky, each stroke powerful enough to bend the treetops below. Scales caught the sunlight and threw it back in flashes of gold and crimson. Even from that distance, she could see the elegant sweep of his neck, the predatory grace in every movement.

Her heart did that stupid fluttering thing it always did when she saw him in his other form.

Sasha ran to the edge of the woods and stopped at a large clearing.

The dragon landed.

The impact shook the ground beneath her feet, sending small animals scurrying from the under-brush. He folded his wings against his massive body, each one easily thirty feet from tip to base. His head, larger than her entire torso, swung toward her with liquid grace. Those familiar golden eyes, now the size of dinner plates, fixed on her with an intensity that made her breath catch.

The first time she'd seen him, she'd been more than a little terrified. Summoning fire with a thought was one thing. But when he did it, Rook still fundamentally seemed human.

When he was the size of a house and covered in scales, it was impossible to forget that he wasn't.

His nostrils flared as he scented the air, and smoke curled from between his teeth in a contented sigh. Sunlight played across his scales, each one perfectly formed, overlapping like armor forged by some cosmic blacksmith. The muscles beneath rippled as he shifted his weight, power contained but never hidden.

You're staring, mate, he whispered in her mind.

The voice was still Rook's, warm and amused, but it carried an undertone of something ancient and wild. The telepathic connection had been startling at first—like having someone else's thoughts suddenly appear in her head—but now it felt as natural as breathing. More intimate than touch, more honest than words.

Yeah, that had also taken some getting used to.

"I can't admire you?"

Her dragon snorted, the sound like steam escaping from a locomotive. Smoke puffed from his nostrils in twin plumes, dissipating in the warm air. His massive head dipped lower, close enough that she could see her reflection in the golden depths of his eyes. Close enough to feel the heat radiating from his scales, warm as a summer day but completely under his control.

He spread out his leg so she had a ramp to climb onto his back.

This part was still kind of terrifying.

The scales beneath her hands were smooth but textured, like touching warm stone that had been polished by centuries of water. Each one was perfectly fitted to its neighbors, creating an armor that looked both beautiful and utterly impenetrable. She could feel the massive muscles beneath his hide, power that could level mountains held in perfect check.

I won't let you fall, he reminded her.

His mental voice carried absolute conviction, the same tone he'd used when promising to protect her from the slavers. When Rook made a promise, the universe itself seemed to bend to make it true.

"There's a first time for everything."

She gripped the ridge of scales along his spine and hauled herself up, her thighs straining as she straddled his broad back. The position put her just behind his shoulder blades, where the powerful wings attached to his torso. She could feel them flexing as he prepared for flight, muscles bunching and releasing in preparation.

Then he was off, launching them into the sky above the woods.

The ground fell away beneath them with stomach-lurching speed. Sasha's hands fisted in the scales at Rook's neck, her knuckles white with the force of her grip. The wind hit her like a physical thing, whipping her hair back and filling her lungs with air so clean it made her dizzy. The trees below shrank to toy-sized models, the clearing where they'd taken off becoming just another patch of green in an endless tapestry of forest.

Rook's wings beat in a rhythm she could feel through her entire body, each downstroke lifting them higher into the crystalline air. The sensation was like riding the world's most powerful motorcycle while strapped to a rocket, terrifying and exhilarating in equal measure. Her stomach dropped with each dip and soared with each rise, leaving her breathless and laughing despite her fear.

The air tasted different up there, thinner and sweeter, carrying scents of flowers and rain from miles away. It filled her nose with the perfume of an entire world, layer upon layer of growing things and clean earth and something indefinable that was purely Vemion. Below them, the forest spread out like a living map, broken by streams that caught the light like silver ribbons and clearings that looked like emerald jewels scattered across green velvet.

Breathe, mate. Rook's mental voice was tinged with amusement. *You're safe.*

Safe. The word should have been ridiculous—she was hundreds of feet in the air with nothing but her grip on a dragon's scales keeping her from plummeting to her death.

But it wasn't ridiculous at all. It was the truest thing she'd ever felt. Rook would die before he let her fall. She knew it in her bones, felt it in the careful way he banked his turns and kept his flight smooth despite the thermals that tried to buffet them.

The fear melted away, replaced by something that felt like pure electricity in her veins. This was flying, real flying, not the cramped metal tube of an airplane but movement through the air as natural as walking. The wind sang in her ears, carrying her laughter back to mix with the whisper of Rook's wings.

It was joy and life personified.

Every cell in her body felt alive, awakened by the rush of wind and the impossible magic of soaring through open sky. Her heart pounded, not with fear now but with exhilaration so pure it bordered on ecstasy.

This was what freedom felt like, not just the absence of constraints, but the presence of infinite possibility stretching out in every direction.

Rook banked left, his wing tip nearly brushing the canopy of a particularly tall tree, and Sasha whooped with delight. The sound was torn away by the wind, but she felt his answering rumble of pleasure through the connection of their bodies. He was showing off for her, she realized, performing aerial acrobatics that probably weren't strictly necessary for transportation. The thought made her heart swell with affection for this powerful creature who still wanted to impress his mate.

The sky above them was the color of forget-me-nots, scattered with wispy clouds that looked close enough to touch. The alien sun warmed her face, different from Earth's star but no less welcoming. This was her world now, her sky, her home.

A year ago, she'd been guiding tourists through familiar forests, her biggest worry whether someone would try to pet a bear. Now she was flying on the back of a dragon lord above an alien world, immune to his fire and bonded to his soul in ways she was still learning to understand.

Her life had become impossible. It had also become perfect.

Wherever her mate asked her to go, she'd say yes.

And she knew she wouldn't regret it.

NEED A LITTLE MORE OF ROOK & SASHA?

Sign up at the link below to **receive a free bonus epilogue!**

Get your free bonus epilogue!

https://katerudolph.net/index.php/rook-bonus/

Thank you so much for reading *Rook*!

Your support means the world to me. If you enjoyed the story, it would mean even more if you could take a moment to share your thoughts in a review or leave a rating.

Hearing from readers like you makes all the difference!

The Dragon Brides series continues with Vex!

WHAT TO READ NEXT: VEX

He's fire and fury. She's the lie that could cost him everything.

Dragon Lord Vex doesn't lose control. Ruthless, disciplined, and sworn to the crown, he's the king's deadliest operative and he has no patience for distractions.

Until Luisa.

She's sharp-tongued, brilliant, and completely off-limits. But to infiltrate a criminal syndicate stealing elite identities from the Intergalactic Dating Agency, Vex has to pretend she's his mistress.

Fake chemistry? No problem.

But it doesn't feel fake.

The heat between them is undeniable. But Luisa's hiding dangerous secrets, and when Vex uncovers the truth, it shatters more than their mission.

Her betrayal cuts deeper than any blade.

His silence hurts more than frostbite.

And the enemy is watching... ready to strike.

With a deadly network closing in, their only hope is each other. But can a dragon who lives by duty risk everything for a woman who breaks all the rules?

One grumpy dragon lord. One secretive human heroine. A fake relationship with scorching consequences.

Fall for the flame in this steamy sci-fi romance packed with enemies-to-lovers tension, undercover intrigue, and heart-melting heat.

Read today!

He's fire and fury. She's the lie that could cost him everything.

Dragon Lord Vex doesn't lose control. Ruthless, disciplined, and sworn to the crown, he's the king's deadliest operative and he has no patience for distractions.

Until Luisa.

She's sharp-tongued, brilliant, and completely off-limits. But to infiltrate a criminal syndicate stealing elite identities from the Intergalactic Dating Agency, Vex has to pretend she's his mistress.

Fake chemistry? No problem.

But it doesn't feel fake.

The heat between them is undeniable. But Luisa's hiding dangerous secrets, and when Vex uncovers the truth, it shatters more than their mission.

Her betrayal cuts deeper than any blade.

His silence hurts more than frostbite.

And the enemy is watching... ready to strike.

With a deadly network closing in, their only hope is each other. But can a dragon who lives by duty risk everything for a woman who breaks all the rules?

One grumpy dragon lord. One secretive human heroine. A fake relationship with scorching consequences.

Fall for the flame in this steamy sci-fi romance packed with enemies-to-lovers tension, undercover intrigue, and heart-melting heat.

INTERGALACTIC DATING
AGENCY

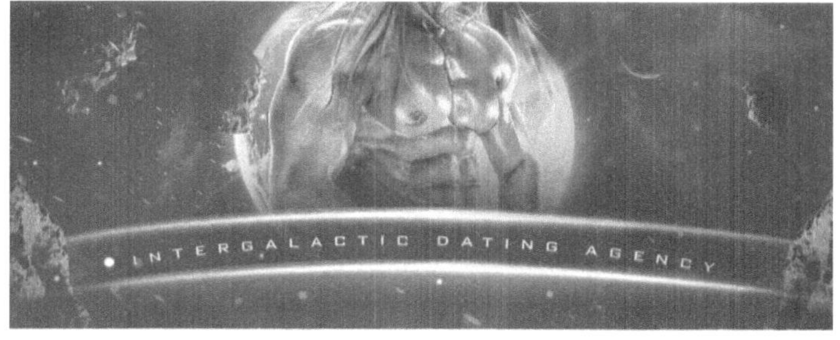

LOOKING for love that's out of this world? These strong, smart, sexy aliens are seeking mates from the Milky Way. Just hop onboard with your local Intergalactic Dating Agency. Join our group of authors as we explore the friendly skies and beyond with trilogies of cosmic craving, astral adventure, and otherworldly lovers. Warning: abductions may or may not be included!

Dragon Brides
Dragon Princes. Fierce Women. Love.
Fated mates, fierce women, and dragon princes are ready to find their mates.

Crux

Ranger

Saber

Cipher

Storm

Drake

Asher

Knox

Flint

Pine

Rook

Vex
Zane

Drakarn Mates
A harsh desert planet. Stranded humans. Draconic aliens. A match made in... well, somewhere.

Claimed by the Drakarn Warrior Lord
Echoes of Fire
Scorched by Fate
Fated to the Drakarn Commander
Chained to the Champion
Beast of Blood and Ash

Guarded by the Shifter

Werewolf. Bodyguard. Mate.
The origins of these shifters are shrouded in mystery, but they're determined to protect their mates from any harm that comes their way.
Also available in audio!

Hunting Season
On the Prowl
Stalking Magic
Hungry for the Wolf
Wolf Cursed (novella)
Wolf's Temptation

Stealing the Alpha

The thief takes what she wants, but the alpha keeps what's his...

Join shifter thief Mel as she clashes with lion alpha Luke in an explosive trilogy of two opposites who can't keep away from one another.

Also available in audio!

The Alpha Heist
Entangled with the Thief
In the Alpha's Bed

Alien Mates: Planet Exile

Guerran is no place for pretty human women. But these alien heroes will protect their mates!
Also available in audio!

Exile's Hunter
Exile's Adored

***

Zulir Warrior Mates

Kidnapped humans. Alien Warriors. Electric wings.
The Zulir Warrior Mates series brings you human heroines and heroes abducted from Earth who find love – and wings! – with the alien warriors who rescue them.
Also available in audio!
Synnr's Saint
Synnr's Hope
Synnr's Spark
Synnr's Kiss
Synnr's Ride

Mated to the Alien

Fated Mate Alien Romance

Detyens are doomed to die young if they don't find their fated mates.

Follow along as these mated pairs fight off aliens, corrupt dictators, prejudiced humans, pirates, and more! The books can be read or listened to in any order, though some characters show up in multiple stories.

Select books available in audio.

Pick a book and jump into the action today!

Ruwen

Tyral

Stoan

Cyborg

Krayter

Kayleb

Shayn

Braxtyn

Doryan

Dekon

Detyen Warriors

Detya was destroyed a hundred years ago. These doomed warriors are out to find justice... and their mates.

The Detyen Warriors series brings you kick butt heroines, alpha alien heroes, fated mates, and relationships strong enough to span the galaxy!

The entire series is also available in audio!

Soulless

Ruthless

Heartless

Faultless

Endless

**Detyen Warrior Outcasts
Fated Mate Alien Romance**

These doomed warriors were abandoned by their people and live on the edge. Their mates hold the key to their salvation.

Pick a book and jump into the action today!

Dangerous Bond

Intrepid Bond

Wayward Bond

Alien Holiday Romance

Christmas... in space????
These alien holiday romances look beyond Earth's winter holidays and ring in the season across the galaxy!
Select titles available in audio.
Snowed in with the Alien Beast
The Alien's Winter Gift
The Alien Reindeer's Wild Ride
Trapped with her Alien Mate

Alien Outlaws

Outlaws, schemes, and love... it's all there in the Alien Outlaws series...
Andie Munster is sick of life on Ixilta, the planet she got dumped on after being abducted from Earth six years ago. And when the mysterious and dangerous Xandr shows up looking for a way off the planet, she's half-prisoner, half-co-conspirator in a wild rush to escape.

Rogue Alien's Escape
Rogue Alien's Woman
Rogue Alien's Secret
Rogue Alien's Legacy

Find more by Kate Rudolph at www. katerudolph.net

ABOUT KATE RUDOLPH

KATE RUDOLPH IS a paranormal and sci-fi romance writer who lives in Indiana. She loves writing about kick butt heroines and the steamy heroes who love them. She's been devouring romance novels since she was too young to be reading them and had to hide her books so no one would take them away. She couldn't imagine a better job in this world than writing romances and sharing them with her fellow readers.

If you enjoyed this story, please consider leaving a review.

9 781953 748805